A Play in Three Acts

by

DAVID ROGERS

TOM JONES

Based upon the Novel by
HENRY FIELDING

THE DRAMATIC PUBLISHING COMPANY

CHICAGO

Notice

TOM JONES

A Comedy in Three Acts
FOR THIRTEEN MEN, ELEVEN WOMEN, EXTRAS
(Can be decreased to ten men, eight women*)

CHARACTERS

PARTRIDGE
BRIDGET ALLWORTHY
SQUIRE ALLWORTHY
DEBORAH
JENNY JONES (MRS. WATERS)
CAPTAIN BLIFIL
BLIFIL
TOM JONES
THWACKUM
SQUARE
MR. WESTERN
SOPHIA WESTERN
MISS WESTERN
HONOUR
JUSTICE DOWLING
DOCTOR

* The characters of Captain Blifil, Thwackum, Square and the Doctor appear only in Act One and the actors who play them can easily double as the Highwayman, who appears only in Act Two, the Constable who is only in Act Three, and Fitzpatrick who is only in Acts Two and Three.

The characters of Bridget Allworthy and Deborah appear only in Act One. Mrs. Whitefield and Susan appear only in Act Two. Lady Bellaston and Nancy appear only in Act Three, and Harriet Fitzpatrick only in Acts Two and Three. These seven roles can easily be covered by four actresses, three if absolutely necessary.

The servants who are used to move furniture throughout the play can be the actresses playing Deborah, Honour, Susan and Nancy. Should the scenery be too difficult for women to manage, men can be dressed to appear as these servants, who do not speak.

3

HIGHWAYMAN
HARRIET FITZPATRICK
FITZPATRICK
MRS. WHITEFIELD
SUSAN
LADY BELLASTON
NANCY
CONSTABLE

THE SCENE: *England.*
THE TIME: *About 1750.*

SYNOPSIS

ACT ONE: *Somersetshire.*

ACT TWO: *The journey.*

ACT THREE: *London.*

4

CHART OF STAGE POSITIONS

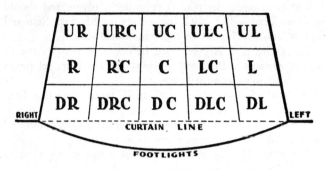

STAGE POSITIONS

Upstage means away from the footlights, *downstage* means toward the footlights, and *right* and *left* are used with reference to the actor as he faces the audience. R means *right*, L means *left*, U means *up*, D means *down*, C means *center*, and these abbreviations are used in combination, as: U R for *up right*, R C for *right center*, D L C for *down left center*, etc. One will note that a position designated on the stage refers to a general territory, rather than to a given point.

NOTE: Before starting rehearsals, chalk off your stage or rehearsal space as indicated above in the *Chart of Stage Positions*. Then teach your actors the meanings and positions of these fundamental terms of stage movement by having them walk from one position to another until they are familiar with them. The use of these abbreviated terms in directing the play saves time, speeds up rehearsals, and reduces the amount of explanation the director has to give to his actors.

PRODUCTION NOTES

SCENERY: Since the play is episodic in nature and should move with movie-like speed, the scenery must be kept light and impressionistic. There is no representational scenery.

The entire play is performed before a blue cyclorama or neutral curtains at the back of the stage. There are set pieces for each act to suggest the locale.

ACT ONE: Somersetshire. Two small cutouts depicting English manor houses in miniature. Placed, one at U R and one at U L, they represent the homes of Allworthy and Western and should look like these houses seen in perspective.

ACT TWO: The Journey. A cutout of a tree at U L C and a moon hung on the back curtain.

ACT THREE: London. A cutout of London Bridge placed U C.

Other than these pieces, there are three movable doors required. They should be practical doors set in door frames and placed on rollers for easy movability. One works as the door to Sophia's room at the beginning of Act Two and all three are used for the Inn at Upton at the end of Act Two. Two are used again in the third act as front doors in London. If actual doors are too difficult to construct, window shades with doors painted on them, hung from wheeled frames resembling—or indeed, actually—clothes racks, may be used. In this case the actors must raise and lower the shades to suggest opening and closing doors.

The rest of the scenery is just furniture: heavier wood pieces for the first two acts which are set in the country and more delicate upholstered pieces for Lady Bellaston's home in London in Act Three.

TEMPO: Nothing adds more to the polish of a production than the quick picking up of cues. Unless there is a definite reason for a pause, train your actors to come in with their speeches "on the heels," so to speak, of the preceding speeches. When a production lags, audience interest likewise will lag. It is always advisable during the last week of rehearsals to hold one or more sessions during which the actors merely sit around in a circle and go through lines only, with the express purpose of snapping up cues.

ACT ONE

SCENE: *When the audience enters the theatre, the curtain is up and the stage is bare except for a blue cyclorama or neutral curtains at the back. There is a small stool* D R *in front of the proscenium.*

AS PLAY OPENS: *When the play is to begin, as the house lights are lowered* PARTRIDGE, *a country man, humbly but neatly dressed, appears. With the help of two or three servants (male or female) dressed in appropriate costumes, he puts up the scenery. This consists of two small cutouts depicting English manor houses set up at back before the cyclorama, the one at the right representing Squire Allworthy's home, the one at* L *the home of Mr. Western. Next, the servants bring in a wooden table and two chairs which they set at* R C. PARTRIDGE *supervises this in pantomime and, when he is satisfied, he waves the servants off. By now, the house lights are off and he advances to the footlights.*

PARTRIDGE. Good evening, my lords, my ladies, gentlemen and gentlewomen and anyone else in hearing of my voice . . . though the Lord alone would know who that might be. Tonight we play "The History of Tom Jones, a Foundling." [*Remembering he must say this.*] Oh, set your minds at rest, good gentle people, I am not regularly an actor. Thank Heaven for small favors. I am your humble servant, Partridge, schoolmaster, surgeon and barber. [*Bows.*] I tell the story of Tom Jones because I know the facts, I have some small part in it, and I am told I have the wit to address so large and distinguished an audience as yourselves . . . but wit is a necessity in a barber. Many people said Tom Jones was born to hang and others called hanging too good for him. But I say, Tom was a paragon of virtue—misunderstood as the good so often are in this wicked world. Our story takes place more than two hundred years ago when the world was, indeed, wicked, bawdy and licentious. In short, a time like any other. But, I am bound to protect innocence and as all here look pure in heart, I shall endeavor to launder the more indelicate passages of this history. [*If the play is* not *to be performed in costume, insert this line:*] Oh, one more thing. Though I, and the other characters in this history, were all born more than two hundred years ago, you will notice that we all dress in modern clothes rather than the costume of our period. This is a conceit of our director, Mr. ...., that not only encourages you to use your imagination, but also greatly lowers the cost of your tickets. So, please to imagine the gentlemen all in breeches and frock coats and the ladies in elaborate gowns. If you wish to save even more money, imagine us in wigs as well. . . . Tom Jones, the foundling, was born—or rather, found —in Somersetshire, one of the green counties of England, in the home—[*He points to it.*]—of Squire Allworthy.

[BRIDGET ALLWORTHY *enters* R. *She is plain, dressed somberly but respectably as befits the gentry.*]

PARTRIDGE. This is the Squire's sister, Miss Bridget Allworthy, a maiden lady of uncertain age. She is to be commended for her good qualities rather than her beauty.

BRIDGET [*to audience*]. I thank Heaven I have not the beauty of the ladies of fashion. Beauty leads a woman to misfortune.

PARTRIDGE [*to* BRIDGET]. Have no fear. [*To audience.*] And this is the Squire himself, returned this very night after an absence of some months.

[*The* SQUIRE *enters* D L. *He is a distinguished man, conservatively dressed.*]

ALLWORTHY [*to audience*]. I thank Heaven for my safe return from London where I can truthfully say they love me just as much as they do in the country for my wisdom, my godliness and my money.

BRIDGET [*crossing to him to begin the scene*]. Welcome home, brother.

ALLWORTHY. Thank you, sister. [*They embrace.*]

PARTRIDGE. The Squire, exhausted . . .

ALLWORTHY [*to* BRIDGET]. I'm exhausted.

PARTRIDGE. . . . retired immediately to his bed chamber— [ALLWORTHY *goes out* D R.]—from which instantly issued a great cry. [PARTRIDGE *sits on stool* D R *and observes the action.*]

ALLWORTHY [*off* R]. Merciful heavens!

BRIDGET [*calling off*]. Brother! What's happened?

[DEBORAH, *an elderly servant, rushes on from* U R.]

DEBORAH. What's happened to the master?

BRIDGET. I don't know. [*Calling off.*] What is it, brother?

[ALLWORTHY *enters, carrying a baby wrapped in a blanket.*]

ALLWORTHY. In my room! A baby!

BRIDGET [*shocked*]. A baby!

DEBORAH. La, Squire, wherever has it come from?

ALLWORTHY [*furious*]. From my pillow.

DEBORAH [*beaming*]. Congratulations!

ALLWORTHY. Nonsense. The child is not mine.

DEBORAH [*instantly serious*]. Of course not, but—[*Wisely.*]— many honest souls will delight in saying it all the same.

ALLWORTHY. What's to be done?

DEBORAH. Put it in a basket and lay it at the churchwarden's door. It's a good night—only a little wind and rain. . . . It is two to one it lives till it be found in the morning.

BRIDGET [*taking baby*]. It is a sweet-looking child.

ALLWORTHY. It must belong to one of the servants.

DEBORAH [*insulted*]. Lud, sir!

ALLWORTHY [*calming her*]. One of the younger servants. Who else could have put it in my room?

BRIDGET. But which one? Polly? Katherine? Jenny?

ALLWORTHY. Yes. Which one, indeed!

DEBORAH. It was Jenny Jones, I'll warrant.

BRIDGET. Jenny Jones!

DEBORAH. She has been seen walking out with the schoolmaster, Mr. Partridge.

PARTRIDGE [*leaping up*]. That's a lie!

DEBORAH. The whole village knows. You've been seen.

PARTRIDGE. I was teaching her Latin and Greek.

BRIDGET. What need has a scullery maid of Greek and Latin?

PARTRIDGE [*piously*]. A knowledge of the classics improves the meanest soul.

ALLWORTHY [*to* DEBORAH]. Bring Jenny Jones to me! [DEBORAH *goes out* U R.]

PARTRIDGE [*to audience*]. It's true Jenny is a scullery maid but she has a good, inquiring mind.

ALLWORTHY [*to* PARTRIDGE]. I am afraid she has inquired too far.

[DEBORAH *returns* U R, *bringing* JENNY, *a pretty girl dressed in rags. Her face is covered with dirt, her straggly hair hangs over it. Since Jenny will appear again under a different name and unrecognized, it is important to cover her face, keep her faced away from the audience and to let her be seen as little as possible.* DEBORAH *pulls her into the room and throws her at Allworthy's feet.*]

ALLWORTHY [*sternly*]. Jenny Jones, are you the mother of that child?

JENNY [*humbly*]. Yes, sir.

ALLWORTHY. Don't deny it.

JENNY. I have not, sir. I brought him to you hoping you would give him a good home. Your kindness, sir, and your money are known throughout the county.

ALLWORTHY. But who is the father?

JENNY. I promise you faithfully one day you'll know, but I am under the most solemn vow to conceal his name at this time.

ALLWORTHY. I demand to know!

JENNY [*entreating* BRIDGET]. Speak for me, madam.

BRIDGET. I entreat you, brother, to help this unfortunate girl.

During your absence she attended me most faithfully in an illness which struck me while you were gone.

ALLWORTHY. For my dear sister's sake and with the goodness for which I am so deservedly known, I will give you the money with which to leave the county, escape your ruined reputation and build a new life elsewhere.

JENNY. Thank you, sir.

ALLWORTHY. And as for your child—[*Takes baby from* BRIDGET.]—I shall provide for him in a better manner than you can ever hope to do.

JENNY. You are too good, sir. [ALLWORTHY *waves her away.* DEBORAH *pulls her out* U R.]

DEBORAH [*as she goes*]. Too good by half.

BRIDGET. You are so good, brother.

ALLWORTHY [*accepting it as a fact*]. Yes. As for the school-master, have him removed from the school and run out of the county or I'll have him strung up by the thumbs. [ALL-WORTHY *exits* R; BRIDGET *exits* L.]

PARTRIDGE [*to audience*]. I was innocent! Innocent! As you shall see. [*Calls to the servants.*] You, there! Take these things away!

[*The servants enter and remove the furniture as he continues.*]

PARTRIDGE. But due to Squire Allworthy's goodness, I was banished from the county anyway. I lost my little school, and was reduced to becoming a barber—and surgeon—and I pulled a tooth now and then to help keep body and soul together. But my part returns to the story later. [*Pause.*] The Squire called the baby "Jones" after Jenny and "Tom" after his own whim. Tom Jones. Shortly after I was banished, a certain Captain Blifil became the guest of Squire All-worthy . . .

[CAPTAIN BLIFIL, *a young man in his twenties, appears* D L.]

PARTRIDGE. . . . and fell in love with his host's sister.

[BRIDGET *appears to the left of the* CAPTAIN *and they hold hands.*]

PARTRIDGE. He was certainly a gallant captain as Miss All-worthy was older than he and—to put it delicately—not the fairest of her sex.

CAPTAIN BLIFIL [*priggishly*]. Beauty is only skin deep and fades as a plucked rose. The deeper qualities such as money and property last forever.

PARTRIDGE. And so they were married—[CAPTAIN BLIFIL *slips a ring on Bridget's finger and they kiss.*]—and a year later, blessed with a fine, bouncing baby boy. [BRIDGET *reaches into the wings and a baby wrapped in a blanket is slipped into her arms. She and the Captain coo at it.*] Not long after, tragedy struck the good captain, who died of an epilepsy or an apoplexy depending upon which doctor you asked. [CAPTAIN BLIFIL *drops his head on his shoulder to symbolize his death.*] Good-by, Captain Blifil.

CAPTAIN BLIFIL. But . . .

PARTRIDGE. You may go. Remember, there are no small parts —only small actors. [CAPTAIN BLIFIL *exits* D L, *followed by* BRIDGET.] And so the two boys grew to manhood. The fatherless Blifil, a serious, studious boy who saved his money and became the most virtuous man in the county, as he was the first to admit . . .

[BLIFIL *appears* R C. *He is serious, sallow, possibly with pimples. He is dressed in black.*]

BLIFIL [*reading from a book he carries*]. Sir Francis Bacon, 1561–1626, said, "Nobility of birth commonly abateth industry." [*Looks up.*] I have proved him wrong. [*Continues to read.*]

PARTRIDGE. While the entirely parentless Tom was a cheery fellow more at home in the woods and fields than with books, who wasted his money in buying food for the starving villagers.

[TOM *appears* D R, *a good-looking fellow in breeches and shirt.*]

TOM. I'm a lucky fellow! The whole world is too good to me.

[*Takes some wood and a knife from his pocket, sits on the floor and whittles.*]

BLIFIL [*looking up for a moment, snarling at* TOM]. Foundling!

PARTRIDGE. The good Squire Allworthy engaged two gentlemen to educate his nephew and his ward. The Reverend Mr. Thwackum . . .

[THWACKUM, *a heavy-set, sanctimonious gentleman, enters* R *and stands behind* TOM.]

PARTRIDGE. . . . a gentleman of great learning and a severe disciplinarian.

THWACKUM. Human nature is the perfection of all virtue.

PARTRIDGE. And Mr. Square, a philosopher.

[MR. SQUARE, *a sour-looking man in black, enters* R, *above* BLIFIL.]

SQUARE. The human mind since the Fall is nothing but a sink of iniquity.

PARTRIDGE. Their contrary teachings did not confuse their pupils, as Mr. Blifil learned everything and could easily discourse on either side, pleasing both his tutors.

BLIFIL [*to* THWACKUM]. God is love.

THWACKUM [*pleased*]. Yes.

BLIFIL [*to* SQUARE]. Science is all.

SQUARE [*pleased*]. Quite.

PARTRIDGE. While Tom—[SQUARE *and* THWACKUM *move to around* TOM.]—listened to neither.

TOM [*still whittling, singing*]. Hey nonny nonny, hey nonny nonny, hey nonny nonny, no! [THWACKUM *and* SQUARE *both hit him.*]

PARTRIDGE [*pointing to Western's house* U L]. On the next estate to Squire Allworthy lived a Mr. Western, a gentleman much given to horses, hounds and hunting.

[MR. WESTERN, *a rather raffish gentleman in a sloppy dark suit and perhaps a mangy, over-curly wig, carrying a pistol, enters* L.]

WESTERN. Tally-ho!

PARTRIDGE. He became a good friend to Tom—[TOM *rises, runs to* MR. WESTERN. *They assume a friendly pose.*]—who had assisted him in a matter concerning poachers.

TOM [*pointing* R]. Over there, sir! [WESTERN *fires a shot. A man screams off* R.]

WESTERN. Got him! That's the last pheasant that peasant will pluck from my preserve.

PARTRIDGE. Tom was a welcome guest at Western's table. Western often declared . . .

WESTERN. Tom Jones will make a great man with any encouragement. I wish I had a son with his parts.

PARTRIDGE. However, Mr. Western had no son. He had a lovely daughter, Sophia.

[SOPHIA, *a very pretty young girl, enters* L *and stands beside her father.*]

WESTERN. A sweet girl, I wouldn't trade her for the best pack of hounds in England.

PARTRIDGE. She was beautiful and modest. She played the pianoforte and sang beautifully . . .

SOPHIA [*singing*]. "Believe me, if all those endearing young charms . . ." [*She goes very flat on the word "charms."*]

PARTRIDGE. . . . for a girl educated in the country. Sophia's mother was long since dead and Western had occasional assistance in the rearing of his daughter from his sister, Miss Western—

[MISS WESTERN *enters* L. *She is an older lady of commanding appearance, dressed in the more fashionable London manner.*]

PARTRIDGE. Who, though a Londoner by preference, made frequent visits to the country to instruct her niece in the manners of the world of fashion.

MISS WESTERN. I am well versed in all the arts which fine ladies use when they desire to give encouragement or to conceal liking. I have instructed my niece in the whole long appendage of—[*Giving examples of each.*]—smiles, ogles, glances and flirtation with her fan.

WESTERN [*annoyed with this*]. Zooks! I say a pox on your flirtation with the fan.

MISS WESTERN [*snapping her fan shut*]. Mr. Western, I think you daily improve in ignorance. [*Goes out* L. THWACKUM, SQUARE *and* BLIFIL *go out* R.]

PARTRIDGE. One day when young Tom had joined Mr. Western and his daughter for a hunt . . . [*Sounds of barking hounds, horses' hoofs.*]

WESTERN [*spying a fox, yelling*]. There she goes! After her! [*Runs, as if on horseback, a complete circle of the stage and then goes out* L. SOPHIA *follows him and* TOM *follows her, but they do not go off but keep circling the stage through the following.*]

PARTRIDGE. I ask you gentle playgoers to imagine them all on horseback. If you are willing to imagine the battle of Agincourt for Master Shakespeare, you can imagine three horses for me. [*Suddenly* SOPHIA *screams and runs faster.*] Miss Sophia lost control of her horse. Young Tom gave chase . . . [TOM *chases.*] . . . leaped off his horse . . . [TOM *pantomimes this.*] . . . the lady's horse reared . . . [SOPHIA *leaps up, then falls on top of* TOM, *both landing in a heap on the ground.*] Delicacy forbids that I overhear what followed. [*Goes out* D R.]

SOPHIA. Why, Tom, you saved my life! [*Looks at him a second, then kisses him.*]

TOM [*drawing away from her kiss*]. No, Miss Western, I cannot take such liberty. [*Rising.*] If I have saved you I am sufficiently repaid, though it cost me greater misfortune than I have suffered on this occasion.

SOPHIA [*also rising*]. What misfortune?

TOM [*phony brave*]. It's nothing. If I have broken my arm, I consider it a trifle compared with what I feared might happen to you. [*Doubles over in pain, groaning.*]

SOPHIA. Broken your arm!

TOM. Do not concern yourself, madam. No doubt it will heal,

[*Groans again.*] But you, you have a small scratch on your forehead . . . it must be attended to. I have a right hand yet at your service to help you to your father's house.

[WESTERN *enters* L.]

WESTERN. What, Sophy? Are you all right?

SOPHIA. Yes. Mr. Jones saved me . . . but he has broken his arm.

WESTERN. Saved my girl! [*Embracing* TOM.] I love you dearly, boy. [TOM *screams in pain.*] What? Does it hurt?

TOM. Only when you thank me.

WESTERN. I'm glad it's no worse. Come back to our house, boy, and if your arm's broken we'll get a barber to join it again.

SOPHIA. But we have no horses . . . and Mr. Jones is injured. Can you not send a carriage back for us?

TOM. Oh, no. Do not trouble yourself, I pray you. It's hardly two miles to your house and such a lovely day I'd rather walk. [*Gestures to* SOPHIA, *indicating she should go. She goes out* U L. WESTERN *throws an arm around Tom's shoulder,* TOM *cries in pain again, then smiles bravely, and they go off after her. A servant enters and places a bench* D L *and exits.*]

[SOPHIA *enters* L *with* HONOUR, *her pretty, young maid.*]

HONOUR. I've just come from the room, Madame. The surgeon has finished with Mr. Jones and Mr. Jones begs me to tell you he will attend you immediately.

SOPHIA [*sitting on bench; in a rapture of love*]. Oh, Honour, is he not the most handsome man you have ever seen in your life?

HONOUR [*being fair*]. Certainly the handsomest man without parents, madam.

SOPHIA [*regretfully*]. It's true he *is* base born . . . but when he smiles . . . he seems . . . almost noble.

HONOUR [*understanding Sophia's sentiments*]. Yes. I could

tell your ladyship something . . . but I'm afraid it might offend you.

SOPHIA. About Mr. Jones? Prithee, tell me. I will know it this instant.

HONOUR. Why, madam, when I came into the room where Mr. Jones and the surgeon were, I had with me this very muff—[*Holds it up.*]—your ladyship gave me but yesterday . . . and to be sure, Mr. Jones took it up and kissed it. I hardly ever saw such a kiss in my life as he gave it.

SOPHIA. And what did he say?

HONOUR. He screamed in pain, madam.

SOPHIA. Screamed?

HONOUR. The surgeon pulled his arm . . . but then he said it was the prettiest muff in the world.

SOPHIA [*fishing*]. I suppose he did not know it was mine?

HONOUR. "La, sir," I said, "you've seen it a hundred times." "Yes," he cried, "but who can see anything beautiful in the presence of your lady but herself?"

SOPHIA. Oh, Tom!

HONOUR. I hope your ladyship won't be offended, for to be sure, he meant nothing by it.

SOPHIA. No . . . nothing, of course. [*Looks at her own muff.*] Honour, my new muff is odious. It is too big for me, I can't wear it. [*Takes it off.*] Till I get another, you must let me have my old one again and you may have this.

HONOUR [*switching muffs*]. An it gives your ladyship pleasure. [*Goes out* L. SOPHIA *looks at the muff, kisses it.*]

SOPHIA [*rapturously*]. Oh, Tom . . . Tom . . .

[TOM *enters* L, *looking weak, his arm in a sling.*]

TOM. Yes?

SOPHIA [*startled*]. Oh! Mr. Jones! Are you well?

TOM. Never better, madam. [*Reels a little.*]

SOPHIA. Your arm?

TOM. A slight—but painful—sprain. It will be better in an hour's time. [*Totters.*]

SOPHIA. You'd best sit down. [*Rises and forces him down on the bench.*]

TOM [*objecting*]. No . . . no . . .

SOPHIA. You would lessen my obligation at having twice risked your life for me.

TOM. Twice?

SOPHIA. Can you have forgotten the day—[*Sits beside him.*] —before I went to stay with my aunt in London . . . that day when you first accompanied Squire Allworthy to my father's house? You brought me a little bird that you had captured from its nest. A beautiful bird who sang so sweetly.

TOM. I remember . . .

SOPHIA. In that instant, I loved—[*Catches herself.*]—the bird. And then, young Blifil, through some misguided sentiment, set it free. In that instant I hated Blifil. The bird flew to a topmost branch beside the brook, you stripped off your coat and climbed the tree, recapturing my little bird. And then the branch broke and you fell with it into the stream.

TOM. My only sorrow is that the water was not deeper that I might have given my life for you.

SOPHIA [*both are a bit over-dramatic*]. Oh, no! You cannot have such contempt of your own life . . . as I regard it highly.

TOM. Oh, Miss Western, can you desire me to live?

SOPHIA. Yes, yes, with all my heart.

TOM. Miss Western . . . Sophia . . . [*Rising and taking her hand.*] My heart overflows. Pardon me, if I am too bold.

SOPHIA [*also rising*]. Mr. Jones, I will not affect to misunderstand you. I understand you too well. But for Heaven's sake, if you have any affection for me, let me retire to my room before the excitement your strong words have caused makes my heart fly quite out of my breast.

TOM. I fear I've said too much.

SOPHIA. Too much . . . too little . . . and too well.

[HONOUR *runs in from* L.]

HONOUR. Mr. Jones! [*They jump apart guiltily.*] Mr. Jones,

they've sent for you. You must return to Squire Allworthy.
He is taken ill. They fear the end is near.

TOM [*bowing to* SOPHIA]. Your humble servant, madam, oh,
your most humble servant. [SOPHIA *utters a little cry and*
HONOUR *helps her out* L. *A servant enters and removes the
bench.* TOM *walks slowly* R.]

[*Other servants enter at* R, *pushing on a small bed on wheels
with* SQUIRE ALLWORTHY *in nightgown and cap in it.* BLIFIL,
SQUARE *and* THWACKUM *follow the bed in and stand upstage of it. The servants, including* DEBORAH, *stand behind
them.* TOM *enters the scene and kneels downstage at the
head of the bed.*]

ALLWORTHY [*weakly, as the others cry*]. My dear friends, my
physician tells me I am in danger of leaving you shortly.
[*They cry more noisily.*] Do not sorrow thus. This is the
best of life, seeing my friends unwilling to part with me.
[*Renewed crying.*] So I want to say a few words about my
will. [*The group brightens considerably.*] To you, dear
friend Thwackum, I have left a thousand pounds.

THWACKUM [*furious, disappointed*]. A thousand pounds!

ALLWORTHY [*misunderstanding his emotion*]. You all know
well my only fault is generosity. And to you, Mr. Square, a
like sum.

SQUARE [*equally injured*]. No more than Thwackum?

ALLWORTHY [*again misunderstanding*]. How lovely is your
wish to share with your friend in sorrow as well as joy. And
to you, Tom Jones, five hundred pounds a year as well as
one thousand pounds in cash.

TOM [*the only one satisfied, crying and kissing his benefactor's
hand*]. You are too good to me . . . too good . . .

ALLWORTHY [*that's true but I can't help it*]. Well. . . .

TOM. And I assure you, sir, how much your generosity makes
me regret this melancholy occasion. Oh, my friend! My
father!

ALLWORTHY [*displeased*]. Hush! You'll start all those nasty
rumors again! And to you, Nephew Blifil, the rest of my

estate save only five hundred pounds a year which is to revert
to you after the death of your mother.

BLIFIL. Why does my mother need five hundred pounds a year?

ALLWORTHY [*assuming he said thank you*]. You are most
welcome. And now, leave me, all . . . I grow weary.

THE SERVANTS [*angry murmuring*]. What about us? I worked
for the old skinflint twenty-five years! To leave us without a
farthing!

ALLWORTHY [*remembering*]. Oh, yes, my faithful servants . . . [*Weakly hands* BLIFIL *a piece of paper.*] You
will find a list of bequests here, nephew, for my servants,
which I am sure you will bestow on them.

BLIFIL. Certainly, Uncle. [*Turns away and rips up the paper.*]

[JUSTICE DOWLING *enters* L. *He is a fussy little man in black
and in a perpetual hurry.*]

DOWLING. Ho! Ho! Is anyone within? Squire Allworthy? [*As
he calls he advances* R *as though walking through a house.*]
Curse me for a fool, delivering messages when I have no
time! [*He has walked to the scene* R *and, as though entering another room:*] Squire Allworthy?

ALLWORTHY [*weakly*]. I can see no one.

DOWLING. I'm Justice Dowlng. I have important business with
you and I have very little time.

ALLWORTHY [*referring to his death*]. You have more time
than I have.

DOWLING. I bring an urgent message.

ALLWORTHY [*to* BLIFIL]. See to it, Nephew. [BLIFIL *takes*
DOWLING U L C *where they stand talking, back to audience.*]

THWACKUM [*to* SQUARE]. A thousand pounds! An outrage!

SQUARE. An insult! Nothing but my extreme poverty could
prevail upon me to accept it.

ALLWORTHY [*mistaking their concern*]. Good friends, do not
stop to thank me. Go, now, all of you. I feel faint. [TOM
remains slumped on the floor at Allworthy's side.
THWACKUM *and* SQUARE *cross* D L. *The servants go off* L,

returning with a few chairs or small sofa and table which they place almost at C.]

[*As this is happening,* TOM *removes his sling and a bouncy little* DOCTOR, *dressed in black, enters* D L *and crosses to* THWACKUM *and* SQUARE.]

DOCTOR [*false cheer*]. And how is my patient this afternoon?

THWACKUM. Miserable!

SQUARE. Stingy!

DOCTOR. But his health? His symptoms?

SQUARE. Doctor, they are all bad.

THWACKUM. I have little hope for him in this world . . . or the next.

DOCTOR [*shocked*]. Merciful Heaven! When I saw him this morning his only complaint was a severe chill. [*Crosses to the sick bed and sits looking at his patient.* DOWLING *and* BLIFIL *turn and walk down toward* THWACKUM *and* SQUARE.]

DOWLING. I must go, sir. I am a circuit judge and there's been a courtroom full of criminals awaiting me at Bath since yesterday. Forgive me for being the bearer of melancholy tidings. Your servant, sir. [*Rushes off* L, *yelling:*] My horse! Quickly, saddle my horse! [BLIFIL *sinks into one of the chairs.* THWACKUM *and* SQUARE *join him.*]

SQUARE. What further unhappy news?

BLIFIL [*pulling out an enormous handkerchief*]. Ah, gentlemen, my mother . . . [*Buries his face in the handkerchief.*]

THWACKUM. Not . . . not dead?

BLIFIL [*looking up*]. Aye, dead . . . at Salisbury. Returning home from London, she was seized with a gout in the head and the stomach which carried her off like—[*Tries to snap his fingers but can't.*]—like a snap of the fingers. [*Buries his head again.*]

SQUARE. Unhappy woman.

BLIFIL [*crying rather falsely*]. Never to enjoy her five hundred pounds a year.

THWACKUM [*comforting him*]. You must try to enjoy it for her.

BLIFIL. Yes. She'd want it that way. [*The three sit, quiet and sad, as the next scene is played.*]

DOCTOR [*to* ALLWORTHY, *as* TOM *watches*]. Say "Ah."

ALLWORTHY. Ah!

DOCTOR [*looking in his throat, happily*]. Ah . . . a very pretty tone. Your pulse? [*Takes Allworthy's wrist, counts.*] Two, four, six, eight. A very lively beat. Your heart? [*Bends down to listen at the right of Allworthy's chest.*]

TOM. But, Doctor, his heart is on the left.

DOCTOR [*angrily, to* TOM]. How unusual! [*Moves his head.*] Ah, yes, there it is. For a moment I feared the worst. [*Listens, then rises.*] The crisis is past. You will be quite all right.

ALLWORTHY. But this pain in my side?

DOCTOR. Pains within the left side are merely vapors and signify nothing.

ALLWORTHY. My pain is on the right side.

DOCTOR. Ah, the right side! That is what we in medicine call right-side vapors. They signify even less. A fortnight's rest in bed, some bread soaked in wine every three hours and a little chicken soup. You will be right as rain before the month is out.

ALLWORTHY. But this morning you told me I was dying.

DOCTOR. We all die a little every day. But—[*Modestly.*]—I have performed another of my miracles, delaying that unhappy event for many years, I trust. Thank Heaven for modern medicine.

TOM. Then he's all right?

DOCTOR. Completely. All he needs is rest. [DOCTOR *pushes the bed off* R.]

TOM [*leaping up in great joy*]. Heigh-ho! And well-a-day! [*Shouts after him.*] Doctor, you deserve a statue erected to you! [*Runs* L *to the other room where* BLIFIL, THWACKUM *and* SQUARE *sit mournfully.*] He's well! The Squire's well!

Banish your long faces. Let joy be unconfined. [*Sings.*] Hey derry down, hey derry down, hey derry down dell!

BLIFIL. Mr. Jones, your behavior is offensive. We are in mourning.

TOM. Well, mourn no longer. The Squire lives. It is the happiest day ever!

SQUARE. You are indecent.

THWACKUM. Sacrilegious.

BLIFIL. My dear mother has gone to her reward.

TOM [*shocked*]. Oh! I beg your pardon. [*Contrite.*] My joy at Squire Allworthy's recovery was so excessive and I had not heard of your loss. [*Puts out his hand to* BLIFIL.] Allow me to offer my condolences.

BLIFIL [*pointedly ignoring his hand*]. It is no wonder the loss of a parent makes so little impression on you. How can you mourn one parent when you yourself from the moment of your birth have lacked both?

TOM. Confound you for a rascal. Do you refuse my hand and insult me with the misfortune of my birth?

BLIFIL. Insult you, sir? I merely call you what you are. A . . .

[PARTRIDGE *pops in* D R.]

PARTRIDGE. Careful here!

BLIFIL. A foundling.

PARTRIDGE. Oh, that's all right. [*Goes out again.*]

TOM. Do you call me a foundling, sir? [*Slaps* BLIFIL. BLIFIL *slaps him back. They fight.*]

SQUARE [*encouraging* BLIFIL]. Hit him! Hit him!

THWACKUM [*likewise*]. Cuff him on the muzzler.

[DEBORAH *enters* D L.]

DEBORAH [*announcing*]. Mr. Western, Miss Western and Miss Sophia.

[WESTERN, MISS WESTERN *and* SOPHIA *enter* D L. DEBORAH *exits.*]

MISS WESTERN [*social charm despite the fight raging on*]. We have come to inquire after Squire Allworthy.

WESTERN [*observing fight*]. Ho! Jolly good fun! [*To* THWACKUM.] Five pounds on Jones! Who's winning? [TOM, *obviously winning, is chasing the cowardly* BLIFIL *around the stage.*]

BLIFIL [*frightened*]. Help me! Help! [THWACKUM *and* SQUARE *each grab one of Tom's arms.*]

SQUARE [*to* BLIFIL]. Hit him.

THWACKUM. Now, you fool! [BLIFIL *tries.* TOM *dodges, despite being held.* SOPHIA, *seeing* TOM *so put upon, gives a little cry and faints.*]

MISS WESTERN [*seeing* SOPHIA *faint*]. Oh! Oh! Oh! Look to my niece. My niece is dead! [*Wrings her hands.*]

TOM [*his attention called to Sophia's faint*]. Miss Western! [*Slips out of the grasp of* THWACKUM *and* SQUARE, *hits* BLIFIL *who falls to the floor, and rushes to* SOPHIA.]

THWACKUM [*disgusted, to* SQUARE]. He's out.

WESTERN [*delighted*]. Good show! [THWACKUM *and* SQUARE *kneel beside* BLIFIL.]

TOM [*beside* SOPHIA, *chafing her wrists*]. Sophia . . . Sophia . . .

MISS WESTERN [*already mourning*]. She was too emotional for one so young. . . .

SOPHIA [*coming to, seeing* TOM; *madly in love*]. Oh, Tom, Tom, my Tom. . . .

WESTERN. He's saved her! Jones has saved my Sophy! That's twice in one day.

TOM [*modestly*]. It's nothing. [BLIFIL *opens his eyes and half rises.*]

THWACKUM. He's coming 'round.

SQUARE. We'll take him to his room. [*He and* THWACKUM *help* BLIFIL *up and out* U L.]

SOPHIA [*to* TOM]. You're . . . you're bruised . . . your face is red . . . and . . . I think your lip's been cut. [*Smooths his ruffled hair.*]

TOM. It's nothing—just a healthy workout . . . but you . . . you are pale. [*To* WESTERN.] By your leave, sir, I'll just escort Miss Western to the garden. The air will restore her.

WESTERN. Zounds! You are a good lad! The preserver of my
  Sophy! [*Embraces* TOM.]

TOM [*screaming in pain*]. My arm! [WESTERN *releases him*.]

MISS WESTERN. But how is the Squire?

TOM. Quite well, madam. Resting in his room. [*To* SOPHIA.]
  Miss Western? [*Offers her his good arm and escorts her
  out* D L.]

MISS WESTERN [*crossing to* WESTERN, *conspiratorially*]. Pray,
  brother, have you not observed something very extraordinary
  in my niece just now?

WESTERN. Is anything the matter with the girl? [*Passionately*.]
  Tell me at once! You know I love my Sophy better than
  my own soul. I shall send to the world's end for the best
  physician.

MISS WESTERN [*laughing*]. Nay, nay, dear brother. You mis-
  interpret me. I meant, I feel my niece to be most desperately
  in love.

WESTERN [*outraged*]. In love without acquainting me! I'll
  disinherit her. I'll turn her out of doors naked without a
  farthing.

MISS WESTERN. But surely you will not turn your daughter,
  whom you love better than your own soul, out of doors before you know whether you approve her choice?

WESTERN. No. If she loves the man I want her to, she may
  love whom she pleases.

MISS WESTERN. Spoken like a sensible man . . . and I believe
  she has chosen the very person you would choose for her.

WESTERN [*impatient*]. But who is the man?

MISS WESTERN [*looking around to be sure she is not over-
  heard, whispering*]. Blifil.

WESTERN [*astounded, thundering*]. *Blifil!*

MISS WESTERN. Shh!

WESTERN [*quietly*]. Blifil?

MISS WESTERN. Did she not faint away on seeing him locked
  in combat?

WESTERN [*amazed*]. 'Fore George, it is certainly so! Ah, my
  sweet Sophy has made a good choice. He has the adjoining

land. Blifil is the perfect estate to marry. What would you
advise me to do?

MISS WESTERN. I think you should propose the match to Allworthy immediately.

WESTERN. But what if he refuses?

MISS WESTERN. Fear not. The match is too advantageous.

WESTERN. I don't know. Allworthy's a queer duck. The money
means little to him.

MISS WESTERN. Brother, I think you are a perfect goat! Do you
think Squire Allworthy has more contempt for money because he professes more?

WESTERN [surprised]. I never thought of it! I'll speak to him
now and bring Blifil back with me.

MISS WESTERN. And I shall inform my niece.

WESTERN [sounding the cry]. Tally ho!

[MISS WESTERN goes out D L. WESTERN crosses R as two servants push Allworthy's bed back on, ALLWORTHY asleep on
it. WESTERN bounces onto the bed.]

WESTERN. Ho, Allworthy! You're looking fit as a hound on
chase! [ALLWORTHY groans.] Well, my old friend. [Slaps
ALLWORTHY on the shoulder.] What think you of my
daughter?

ALLWORTHY [weakly]. Would you mind not bouncing on
the bed?

WESTERN [rising]. Zooks! Curse me for a clumsy oaf!

ALLWORTHY [hand to head]. And . . . please . . . lower
your voice.

WESTERN. I'm not a courtly man, you understand. I do not
take to the fashionable way, but I say what I mean. What
say you to a match between my daughter and your nephew?

ALLWORTHY [sitting up, greedily pleased]. How very advantageous. It would combine our estates. [Suddenly remembering his manners and his health he lies down again.
Weakly:] She's a charming girl, charming. [To the servants.] Send Mr. Blifil to me. [The servants go out R.]

[WESTERN *sits on the bed and the two men continue their conversation in pantomime as* MISS WESTERN, *arm around* SOPHIA, *enters* D L.]

MISS WESTERN [*continuing a conversation*]. . . . and so, Sophia, though you have tried to hide your feelings, your clever aunt has seen through you. In a word, niece, I know you are in love.

SOPHIA [*horrified at the discovery*]. Oh, madam!

MISS WESTERN. Blush not, my gentle Sophia. Your father and I entirely approve your choice. Your father is with Squire Allworthy proposing the match.

SOPHIA. Now?

MISS WESTERN. You know the impetuosity of my brother's temper. [*They sit on sofa.*] As soon as I acquainted him with your passion, which I discovered the moment that you fainted, he went to Allworthy. He should be back with your lover within five minutes. You are to put on all your best airs.

SOPHIA. Five minutes! Dear Aunt, you frighten me out of my senses.

MISS WESTERN. You'll soon come to yourself again, for he is a charming young man—that's the truth on't.

SOPHIA. Nay, I admit, I know none with such perfections. So brave . . .

MISS WESTERN. And yet so gentle.

SOPHIA. So witty . . .

MISS WESTERN. Yet so inoffensive.

SOPHIA. So humane, so civil, so handsome.

MISS WESTERN. Yes, yes. True, true.

SOPHIA. What does it signify that he is base born?

MISS WESTERN [*leaping up in horror*]. Base born! Base born! What do you mean, calling Mr. Blifil base born?

SOPHIA [*leaping up in horror in her turn*]. Mr. Blifil!

MISS WESTERN. Yes, Blifil! Of whom else have we been talking?

SOPHIA. Of Mr. Jones, I thought.

MISS WESTERN [*reaching new crescendos of horror*]. Mr. Jones! Is it possible that you can think of disgracing your family by allying yourself with a foundling? I wonder you have the courage to admit it to my face.

SOPHIA. Madam, you tricked this admission from me. I had intended to carry my thoughts of Mr. Jones with me to a maiden's grave.

MISS WESTERN. I would rather follow you to the grave alone than to the altar with Mr. Jones. Oh, heavens! Your father will probably set the dogs on you . . . unless he's really angry, and then he might do worse.

SOPHIA [*frightened*]. I beseech you not to tell him.

MISS WESTERN. I will keep your secret on one condition. That you see Mr. Blifil. That you are civil to Blifil. And that you regard him as the person who is to be your husband. Otherwise, let my brother do his worst.

SOPHIA. I am forced to agree . . . but will you not speak to my father and try to change his mind? To be Mrs. Blifil is to be the unhappiest woman alive.

MISS WESTERN. No, Sophia. On the contrary, I will do all I can to put your honor out of the care of your family. Remember, marriage has saved many a woman from ruin. [*Crosses* R.] I go to raise up Blifil to the attack—metaphorically speaking. [*Rushes to Allworthy's bedroom.* SOPHIA *sinks, in tears, to a chair and cries quietly as the following scene progresses.*]

[*As* MISS WESTERN *joins* WESTERN *and* ALLWORTHY *from the* L, BLIFIL, *an enormous black-bordered handkerchief to his eyes, enters* R.]

BLIFIL [*to* ALLWORTHY]. Oh, sir, unhappy news. My dear Mamma is lost on the road from London.

ALLWORTHY. Lost! Bridget! Your mother is an excellent needlewoman but she has no sense of direction.

BLIFIL. Not lost upon the road! Lost to this world. Carried off by a severe gout in the head and the stomach.

ALLWORTHY. How very unfortunate.

WESTERN. Ay. She should never have gone to London. The air is enough to kill a stronger body.

MISS WESTERN [*rising to London's defense*]. London is not to blame. Remember, she died in the country . . . upon leaving London.

WESTERN [*ready to fight*]. It was London, I say . . .

ALLWORTHY [*interrupting*]. Please . . . we will mourn Mrs. Blifil later. To the matter at hand. My physician says I must have rest.

WESTERN. Ay. Get on with it.

ALLWORTHY. Nephew, have you thought of marrying?

BLIFIL. No.

ALLWORTHY. I am happy to hear it. Our good neighbor, Mr. Western, has offered you his daughter Sophia in marriage. I have, of course, accepted.

BLIFIL. But, Uncle, I am too young to marry . . . and too recently bereaved. [*Touches his eyes with his handkerchief.*]

ALLWORTHY. Nonsense! It will make a man of you.

BLIFIL. But . . .

WESTERN. My Sophia is as pretty as a nestin' partridge.

BLIFIL. But . . .

MISS WESTERN. She plays and sings with a true voice.

BLIFIL. But . . .

ALLWORTHY. She is charming and gay.

BLIFIL. But . . .

WESTERN. She rides near as good as a man.

BLIFIL. But . . .

MISS WESTERN [*firmly*]. She is very, very rich!

BLIFIL [*at once, to* ALLWORTHY]. I shall in all things do what will give you pleasure, Uncle.

WESTERN. I'll tell Sophy it's settled.

ALLWORTHY. Good. The doctor says I must have rest. Nephew . . . [*Gestures, and* BLIFIL *and* MISS WESTERN *push the bed out at* R. WESTERN *crosses to* SOPHIA, *who is still crying.*]

WESTERN. Come, my girl. No tears. None of your maidenish airs. My sister has told me all.

SOPHIA [*a little cry*]. Then my aunt has betrayed me? I am undone!

WESTERN. Why, you betrayed yourself, girl, fainting like a very woman. And now crying because you're going to marry the man you love. Women are all alike. Your mother, I remember, whimpered and whined when we were wed. But twenty-four hours later, it was all over. She rarely made a sound again. So, cheer up. Mr. Blifil is a brisk young man and will soon put an end to your squeamishness.

SOPHIA [*relieved*]. Blifil! She told you about Blifil!

WESTERN. I'll call him to you. [*Bellows off* R.] Blifil! Let's get on with it!

[BLIFIL *appears at* R *and crosses toward them.*]

WESTERN. Here he is, girl. Blifil. [WESTERN *goes out* D L. SOPHIA *looks away from* BLIFIL.]

BLIFIL. Miss Sophia?

SOPHIA [*turning to him, coldly*]. Yes?

BLIFIL [*formally*]. My uncle has informed me that he and your father have decided we should be wed. I am most pleased.

SOPHIA [*sarcastic*]. Your emotion overwhelms me.

BLIFIL [*speaking words he feels he should; no emotion at all*]. The thought of our future bliss has, I fear, aroused the beast in me.

SOPHIA [*hating him but playing her part*]. La, Sir! You are forward. You shock me!

BLIFIL [*crossing to her*]. I want only to express my joy at the merging, if I may so put it, of our souls and our estates. [*Takes her hand and shakes it.*]

SOPHIA [*withdrawing her hand, angrily*]. You take too many liberties, sir.

BLIFIL. I beg your pardon.

SOPHIA [*furious*]. Leave me now, lest the passion I feel should begin to overcome me.

BLIFIL [*surprised*]. Passion? For me?

SOPHIA. Let us just say passion. [*In no uncertain tone.*] Leave,
now.

BLIFIL. Your servant, madam.

[BLIFIL *bows and crosses* L, *meeting* WESTERN, *who enters*
D L.]

WESTERN. Well?

BLIFIL. She's mad about me. [*Goes out* L. WESTERN, *delighted,
crosses to* SOPHIA.]

WESTERN [*kissing her*]. Ah, Sophy, girl, ask what you will.
Dresses . . . furs . . . livestock. . . . I have no fortune
but to make you happy.

SOPHIA [*her pent-up feelings exploding*]. No, *no, no, no, no,
no!* I cannot live with Mr. Blifil.

WESTERN [*booming into a rage*]. Cannot live with Blifil! Then
die, and a pox on you!

SOPHIA. I hate and detest him!

WESTERN. No matter how much you detest him, you shall have
him. I am resolved, and unless you consent, I will throw you
starving into the streets.

[SOPHIA *bursts into tears*. WESTERN *stalks off* L, *meeting* TOM,
who enters D L, *having put on cravat, waistcoat and coat.*]

TOM. Has Miss Western recovered?

WESTERN. Recovered? Ay, from her fainting fit, she has recovered. But now she has gone quite mad!

TOM [*upset*]. Mad! Can this be?

WESTERN. So mad, so willful she would disobey the sweetest,
most generous, most understanding father in the country.
[*Screaming.*] She will not marry Blifil!

TOM [*horrified*]. Marry Blifil! Is that what you wish?

WESTERN [*pulling himself together*]. I am in too great a passion to speak. I shall walk by the stables. The smell of the
horses may calm me. Oh, Tom Jones, my good companion
on many a hunt, go, prithee, talk to her. See what you can
do. Oh, Ingratitude! Oh, Disobedience! [*The final insult.*]

She's just like her mother! [WESTERN *goes out* D L. TOM *crosses to the weeping* SOPHIA.]

TOM. Oh, my Sophia, I know. Your cruel father has told me all and sent me hither to you.

SOPHIA. Sent you to me?

TOM. To plead with you for my odious rival, Blifil. Forgive me for mentioning his name.

SOPHIA. It is his person I object to, not his name. What's in a name? That which we call garbage by any other name would smell.

TOM. Sophia, oh, Sophia, in a moment we may be torn apart forever. Nothing less than this cruel occasion could make me brave enough to speak.

SOPHIA. What would you say?

TOM. Promise me you will never marry Blifil.

SOPHIA [*promising*]. Never.

TOM. And add that I may hope.

SOPHIA. What hope can I bestow? My own ruin will be the consequence of my disobedience. And think of the ruin I must bring on you should I comply with your desire.

TOM. I love you.

SOPHIA. Oh, no! Fly from me forever and avoid your own destruction.

TOM. I fear no destruction but the loss of my Sophia. I can never part with you. I will never part from you. [*They kiss and hold the kiss through the following.*]

[MISS WESTERN *and* WESTERN *enter* D L.]

MISS WESTERN [*outraged*]. You have left my niece alone with Jones?

WESTERN. Perhaps he can persuade her to marry Blifil.

MISS WESTERN [*the end of her rope*]. Oh, more than Gothic ignorance! You country oaf! You bucolic clod! 'Tis Jones she loves.

WESTERN [*beside himself*]. Jones! I'll have his heart! [*Runs to* TOM *and* SOPHIA, *screaming.*] Sophia! [*The lovers jump apart.* MISS WESTERN *comes up behind* WESTERN. *To* TOM:]

You scoundrel! I will have satisfaction of you! [*Throws off his coat.*] I'll lick you as well as you were ever licked in your life.

TOM [*bravely*]. I will not lift my hand against the father of Sophia.

WESTERN. Serpent! Swine! You perfect villain! Do not add cowardice to your many other faults.

[THWACKUM *and* SQUARE *enter* U L.]

THWACKUM *and* SQUARE. What is it? What's all this pother?

[ALLWORTHY, *still in his night clothes, enters* D R, *hobbling weakly on* BLIFIL'S *arm.*]

ALLWORTHY [*walking into scene*]. What's this row? There's too much noise. My doctor says I must have rest.

WESTERN [*enraged*]. A nasty piece of work! My daughter has fallen in love with your foundling.

ALLWORTHY. Good heavens!

BLIFIL. She can't love Jones. He hasn't a penny.

MISS WESTERN. Spoken like a true romantic.

THWACKUM *and* SQUARE. Hear! Hear!

BLIFIL. She would be dragged down to the very gutter were she to marry that foundling, who, though I have managed to conceal the fact from you, dear Uncle, is the worst man in the world.

SOPHIA. You lie!

ALLWORTHY. Has he done worse than I already know? Tell me. I command you.

BLIFIL. Wild horses will not drag his evil deeds from me . . . *but* . . . I must obey you in all things, dear Uncle.

WESTERN. Well? Spit it out! What's he done?

BLIFIL. Well, beyond his poaching . . .

WESTERN [*outraged*]. Poaching!

TOM. That's not true!

BLIFIL. And beyond his eying of wenches in the village . . .

MISS WESTERN [*shocked*]. Wench-eying!

TOM. I never. . . . I love but one . . .

BLIFIL. This very day, when you, dear Uncle, lay at death's door, when myself and these good gentlemen—[*Indicating* THWACKUM *and* SQUARE.]—were in tears, he filled the house with riot and debauchery.

TOM. You're lying! Lying!

BLIFIL. He sang and roared . . .

TOM. I sang with happiness at your recovery, dear protector.

BLIFIL. And when I gave him a gentle hint of the indecency of his actions, he fell into a violent passion, swore many oaths and struck me.

ALLWORTHY [*to* TOM]. You struck him?

TOM. Yes, but . . .

BLIFIL [*prissily*]. Of course I forgave him for I have always loved him like a brother, but it grieves me to admit he is a profligate wretch!

TOM [*jumping at* BLIFIL]. You lie! [*Hits* BLIFIL, *who falls.*]

BLIFIL [*almost while falling*]. I forgive him! [THWACKUM *and* SQUARE *rush to attend him.*]

MISS WESTERN. Oh, saintly Blifil.

WESTERN. 'Tis Blifil you will marry.

SOPHIA. Never! Never! With all my heart!

WESTERN. Take her home, sister. Lock her in her room. No meat, no drink till she agrees. [MISS WESTERN *grabs* SOPHIA *by the arm.*]

ALLWORTHY [*to* TOM]. And you, sir, to whom I have shown the kindness and fairness and generosity for which I am renowned . . .

THWACKUM, SQUARE *and* BLIFIL. Renowned! Renowned!

ALLWORTHY. This . . . this is how my charity is repaid?

TOM. Sir, I must follow where my heart leads me. I love Sophia.

MISS WESTERN. Remember your birth, sir. You cannot have the effrontery to love above your station.

ALLWORTHY. I am resolved to banish you forever from her sight and mine.

TOM. Oh, no! Do not exile me from the company of the two human beings I love most in this world.

ALLWORTHY. You will leave my house immediately and never
   return.

SQUARE. Very fair.

THWACKUM. Very just.

BLIFIL. More than kind.

SOPHIA. Tom! Tom!

WESTERN [*to* MISS WESTERN]. Take her out of here! [*As* MISS
   WESTERN *pulls her* L, SOPHIA *looks longingly back to* TOM.]

TOM. Farewell, Sophia. Try to forget me. Farewell. [*Walks out
   of the scene to downstage. The other actors freeze.* TOM
   speaks to the audience.] Where shall I go? What is the
   deepest, darkest, dirtiest hole where I can live out my miserable life in the deepest degradation? There's only one
   choice. I'll go to London. Farewell, Sophia, most lovely,
   most beloved . . . [*Starts walking* R, *as:*]

CURTAIN

ACT TWO

SCENE: *The cutout houses and furniture from the end of Act One have been removed. A small dressing table and chair are set at C. Sophia's muff is on the table. Up above them, there is a clothes tree holding two capes. At L C a door on wheels, the door to Sophia's room, is set perpendicular to the footlights.*

AT RISE OF CURTAIN: SOPHIA *is seated at the table.* MISS WESTERN *is pacing the room haranguing her and* WESTERN *is leaning against the door, listening.*

MISS WESTERN. Don't argue with me, child. You are to consider me as Socrates, not asking your opinion but only informing you of mine.

SOPHIA. I have never presumed to question your opinion, madam, save only on this topic of marriage.

MISS WESTERN. Matrimony is not a romantic scheme of happiness arising from love. It is a fund in which a prudent woman deposits her fortunes in order to receive the largest possible interest for them.

SOPHIA. But I have no wish to elect Mr. Blifil my bank manager. I hate him.

MISS WESTERN. That is no objection to marrying him. I know many couples who entirely dislike each other and lead very comfortable, genteel lives.

SOPHIA. I am resolved against Mr. Blifil.

WESTERN [*coming forward*]. Resolved, my foot! I say you shall marry him, and marry him you shall. That's all.

MISS WESTERN. Brother, kindly cease your interference. This is a woman's matter and I cannot express the contempt I have for your manners.

WESTERN. A pox on my manners! No wonder I am undervalued by my daughter when she hears the way you speak to me.

36

MISS WESTERN. It is impossible—impossible to undervalue such a boor.

WESTERN. A country boor, madam, who gets to the heart of the matter with none of your London shilly-shally. As for you, daughter, you marry Blifil tomorrow.

SOPHIA [*horrified*]. Tomorrow!

WESTERN. And remain locked in this room with nothing but bread and water till then! Come, Madame Socrates. [*Opens the door for* MISS WESTERN, *who goes through it. He follows.*]

[HONOUR *enters* D L, *carrying a tray with two plates and a mug on it.* WESTERN *takes a large, old-fashioned key from his pocket, then seeing* HONOUR, *says:*]

WESTERN. What's that?

HONOUR. My lady's supper . . . a scrap of yesterday's roast.

WESTERN [*taking one plate*]. I said bread and water! [*Throws the key on the tray.*] See you lock her in when she's finished and return the key to me.

MISS WESTERN. She should have air . . . for her complexion.

WESTERN. Faugh! [*Stalks off* D L, *followed by* MISS WESTERN. HONOUR *goes through door to* SOPHIA.]

SOPHIA. Oh, Honour, Honour, I am undone. What will happen to me?

HONOUR. In the end, my lady, I suppose you'll marry Mr. Blifil. [*Sets the tray on the table.*]

SOPHIA. What's that?

HONOUR. Your supper, my lady.

SOPHIA [*giving it a quick glance*]. Ich!

HONOUR. And if not Blifil, there's not a man in this county or the next who would not be glad to take his place. Why not marry young Squire Edgerton in the next village?

SOPHIA. Oh, Honour, you will not understand! It is not a question of who but Mr. Blifil to marry. It is a question of how to marry Mr. Jones. [*Seeing key on tray, she picks it up.*] Honour, is this the key to my dungeon?

HONOUR. Yes, madam. I am to return it to your father when
    you finish your bread and water.

SOPHIA [*holding key, determined*]. I am come to a resolution.
    I shall follow Mr. Jones to London.

HONOUR [*shocked*]. London! La, madam, how do you know
    he went there?

SOPHIA. Where else is there?

HONOUR [*answering honestly*]. Brighton, Bristol, Canter-
    bury . . .

SOPHIA. Be quiet! You sound like a crier for a stage coach
    line!

HONOUR [*on her own train of thought*]. Has your ladyship
    thought to marry Mr. Fordyce who hunted with your father
    in the spring?

SOPHIA [*on her track*]. I'll go to Lady Bellaston's in London.
    She is a relation of mine who has often begged me to come
    and stay with her. Once there it will be easy to find Mr.
    Jones.

HONOUR [*still encouraging*]. He's a handsome man . . . Mr.
    Fordyce . . .

SOPHIA. Be quiet! I am resolved we are going!

HONOUR [*shocked*]. We? Oh, madam, Mr. Western would
    have me hanged for stealing off with his own daughter.

SOPHIA [*taking a large scarf from table drawer and wrapping
    some jewels and clothes in it*]. Honour, I have some money
    and some few jewels. I will reward you to the very utmost
    of my power.

HONOUR [*greedy*]. The utmost?

SOPHIA. The utmost!

HONOUR. La, madam, how can I refuse the sweetest, dearest,
    most *generous*—[*She underlines that.*]—mistress in the
    world? I know where we can hire a carriage in the next
    village.

SOPHIA [*embracing her*]. Oh, my gentle Honour! [*An idea.*]
    Perhaps I'll steal one of my father's pistols.

HONOUR [*holding* SOPHIA]. And perhaps some of the silver
    and plate?

SOPHIA [*changing her mind*]. No! I'll take nothing! I go to
Mr. Jones as a future wife, not as a highwayman!

HONOUR [*disappointed*]. Well . . . if you're determined.
[SOPHIA *gets her cape and* HONOUR *hers from clothes tree.
As they slip them on:*]

SOPHIA. They'll all be at supper. We can sneak quietly out of
the house.

HONOUR [*one last thought*]. What say you to my Lord Hamp-
ton?

SOPHIA. Nonsense! [*Snatches up the scarf and walks through
the door.*]

HONOUR [*following her*]. Heaven protect us in this venture.

SOPHIA [*suddenly remembering, running back to dressing table*]. My muff! The muff that Mr. Jones has kissed . . .
personally! [*Takes it and runs off* D L, *followed by* HON-
OUR.]

[PARTRIDGE *appears* D R.]

PARTRIDGE [*to audience*]. Hey day! I warrant you forgot I was
here! [*Calls off.*] Hi there! You servants! Clear away all
this stuff!

[*The servants come on and clear away Sophia's room and door
as* PARTRIDGE *talks to the audience.*]

PARTRIDGE. I beg your pardon, sirs and ladies, I was supposed
to introduce the first part of this act but I was detained back
there—[*Points off.*]—by important matters of business.

WOMAN'S VOICE [*off* R]. You villain!

PARTRIDGE [*embarrassed, calling off*]. Now, now, love! Not
in front of all these people. [*To audience.*] Well, here we
are in Part Two of our story. I call it "The Journey" for it's
the part where Tom goes from Somersetshire to London.
[*Looks to see what servants have done. By now they should
have cleared everything.*] You have everything all set now?
Oh, you've forgotten the tree. [*He crosses* R.] I vow if you
don't do everything yourself . . . [*Disappears for a second
and comes back carrying cutouts of a tree and a moon under*

his arm. He takes the tree to U C, *talking all the while.*]
You see they forgot to put the tree up, and without the tree
how are you supposed to know we're out in the open air?
But you just can't get decent help in these terrible times!
You know what I mean? [*Getting the tree set.*] There!
Now this is a road. [*He hangs the moon on the back drop.*]
At night. [*Crosses to his stool* D R *and sits.*]

[TOM *enters* D L. *He carries a knapsack and a large wooden
staff. He is walking. As* PARTRIDGE *speaks, he crosses from*
L *to* R.]

PARTRIDGE. There's Jones. He's been walking a few days now.
He's had a lot of adventures but they don't really have too
much to do with the story, so I skipped 'em. [*Confiden-
tially.*] Y'see, the fellow who wrote this . . . Mr. Fielding
. . . he wrote a lot of stuff he didn't need. Eight hundred
and fifty pages! Wow! That's a lot of parchment.

TOM [*stopping at* R C, *looking at moon*]. Who knows but the
loveliest creature in the universe may have her eyes now
fixed on that very moon which I behold at this instant? Oh,
how I wish that moon was a looking glass and my dear
Sophia was placed before it.

PARTRIDGE [*touched, isn't that sweet*]. Ahhhh.

MRS. WATERS [*a voice from off* U L, *screaming, calling*]. Help
. . . help . . . murder . . . oh, help! [TOM *runs upstage
to see what's happennig.* PARTRIDGE *exits* R.]

[MRS. WATERS, *once known as Jenny Jones, runs on at* U L.
*She is about forty, attractive but currently disheveled, with
her clothing ripped, her hair flying. She is followed by a*
HIGHWAYMAN, *wearing a black cape and a mask and pointing a pistol at her.*]

HIGHWAYMAN [*catching her arm*]. Your money or your life!

MRS. WATERS. Oh, sir, I have no money and, Heaven knows,
a wretched life! [*Pulls away from him and runs, circling
the stage crying:*] Help . . . help . . . murder . . . rob-

bery . . . [HIGHWAYMAN *chases her, and* TOM *falls into step, running along beside* MRS. WATERS.]

TOM. Excuse me, madam, but is this man annoying you?

MRS. WATERS [*running*]. Yes, sir. Most assuredly.

TOM [*running*]. May I be of service?

MRS. WATERS [*running*]. Please . . . [TOM *stops running and faces* HIGHWAYMAN.]

TOM. Hold, you rascal! [*Knocks gun from* HIGHWAYMAN'S *hand with his staff.* MRS. WATERS *cringes behind* TOM.]

HIGHWAYMAN. That's not fair! You have a stick!

TOM. You had a pistol!

HIGHWAYMAN [*like a spoiled child*]. Yes. It's mine! Give it back!

TOM. I shall waste no time with you. Quick justice is required. [*Raises the staff to hit* HIGHWAYMAN. HIGHWAYMAN *grabs the other end. They wrestle for the stick.* HIGHWAYMAN *pulls it away from* TOM.]

HIGHWAYMAN. Ahah! [*Lifts it high.* MRS. WATERS *screams.* HIGHWAYMAN *brings staff down on Tom's head.* TOM *crumples.*] That, varlet, will teach you not to meddle with "The Black Shadow"! [*Turning to* MRS. WATERS.] And, now, madam . . . [MRS. WATERS *makes a frantic grab for the pistol, gets it and points it at him.*]

MRS. WATERS. Stand, sir, or I'll fire.

HIGHWAYMAN [*very nervous*]. Put that thing down! Women are dangerous with firearms.

MRS. WATERS. I shall count to three and fire.

HIGHWAYMAN. No, no. You're supposed to be a defenseless woman who will easily surrender her jewels.

MRS. WATERS. One . . .

HIGHWAYMAN. I did exactly as my master taught. I hid behind a tree, I stopped your horse, I pulled you from him and slapped him down the road . . .

MRS. WATERS. Two . . .

HIGHWAYMAN. True, it's my first job, but I was the best apprentice at the school.

MRS. WATERS. Three! [HIGHWAYMAN *screams and runs off* R.

MRS. WATERS *runs to* TOM, *sits on the ground, cradles his head in her lap. He is beginning to come around.*] Oh, thank you, gentle sir, you saved me!

TOM [*modestly*]. It was nothing.

MRS. WATERS. What might have befallen me had you not happened along. [*Looking at his head.*] Oh! I'm afraid that knave has cracked your head.

TOM [*wondering*]. I've had more accidents these last few days than ever in my life.

MRS. WATERS. I'll bind it till we can find a surgeon. [*Turns and rips the bottom off her dress or petticoat.*]

TOM. You'll ruin your dress.

MRS. WATERS. It's ruined already. La! What must you think of me, sir, dressed like this. I assure you I am usually most fashionable.

TOM [*gallantly*]. I can hardly believe, madam, that anyone could look more lovely than you do now.

MRS. WATERS [*gurgling*]. Oh, sir . . . [*Makes a mild attempt to straighten her hair.*] You *are* a gentleman.

TOM. How came you here in such a predicament?

MRS. WATERS [*as she bandages his head*]. My name is Mrs. Waters. My husband . . .

TOM. Oh! You are married?

MRS. WATERS [*demurely*]. Widowed.

TOM. Oh, I beg your pardon.

MRS. WATERS. Not at all. It's all so long ago. He died . . . it must be . . . it must be 'way last Tuesday.

TOM. My condolences, madam.

MRS. WATERS. Do not think me indifferent and hard, sir, but I have not seen my husband these last seven years. He was a captain in the army.

TOM [*touched*]. He died in the service of his king.

MRS. WATERS. Oh, no, sir! He died in Brighton. Of overeating. He was always too fond of sea food. I was on my way thence . . . to settle his estate . . . when accosted by that highwayman. [*Finishes the bandage.*] There. That will do for the moment, till we can find a surgeon.

TOM [*rising*]. But where can I escort you that you may find
another gown?

MRS. WATERS [*as* TOM *helps her up*]. I believe there is an Inn
at Upton . . . just over this hill.

TOM [*offering her his arm*]. If you will permit me . . .

MRS. WATERS [*taking arm*]. La, sir! How gallant you are.
[*They start off* L. *Romantically:*] Aye me, it is seven years
since last I saw my husband.

[*They walk off* L, *having forgotten staff and pistol. As they
go,* HIGHWAYMAN *returns from* R, *looking for the pistol.*]

HIGHWAYMAN [*mumbling*]. They may have left it . . .
[*Looking.*] I'd be so embarrassed to go back without my
pistol. . . . curse this darkness! [*Removes his mask, the
better to see. He continues looking.*]

SOPHIA [*a voice off* R]. The coachman said the Inn was this
way . . . [HIGHWAYMAN *quickly replaces his mask. He is
now* U L.]

[SOPHIA *and* HONOUR *enter* D R. SOPHIA *carries her scarf and*
HONOUR *a small bag.*]

SOPHIA . . . just over this little hill.

HONOUR. It's cruel that we must walk.

SOPHIA. It's only a few steps. The bridge was down and the
coach too large for this path. [HIGHWAYMAN *advances down
to* SOPHIA, *stops in front of her.*]

HIGHWAYMAN. Your money or your life! [HONOUR *screams.*]

SOPHIA [*startled*]. What? [*Observing and dismissing him.*]
But you don't even have a firearm. [HIGHWAYMAN *looks
down at his hands, realizes, snaps his fingers.* SOPHIA *walks
imperiously around him toward* L, *with* HONOUR *trailing
her.* HIGHWAYMAN *goes upstage, continuing his search.*]

HONOUR. What about Lord Chatsworth, who lives t'other side
of Tunbridge Wells?

SOPHIA. Honour, you're making my head ache.

[HARRIET FITZPATRICK, *an attractive young gentlewoman, enters* D R, *carrying a traveling bag.*]

HARRIET [*calling to* HIGHWAYMAN]. Oh, sir, is this the road
to the Inn at Upton? [*On hearing her voice* HONOUR *and*
SOPHIA *stop* D L. HIGHWAYMAN *turns, runs down to* HAR-
RIET *from* U C.]

HIGHWAYMAN. Your money or your life!

HARRIET [*screaming*]. Merciful heavens!

SOPHIA. Pay no attention to him, dear madam. He has no
weapon and can do you no harm.

HARRIET. That voice! Are you not Sophia Western?

SOPHIA [*recognizing Harriet's voice*]. Why, I do believe . . .
Harriet! Harriet Fitzpatrick! [*The two girls, ignoring the
highwayman, cross and embrace in front of him.*] Dear,
dear cousin.

HARRIET. My sweet Sophia. What a fortunate meeting.

SOPHIA. Indeed, delightful.

HIGHWAYMAN [*an agonized cry*]. What do I do wrong? [*They
ignore him. He listens to their conversation with interest.*]

SOPHIA. I have not seen you since your marriage.

HARRIET. Oh, that unhappy day! Sophia, I have run away
from Mr. Fitzpatrick.

HIGHWAYMAN [*disgusted*]. Run away from your husband!
That's the new morality for you!

SOPHIA [*to* HIGHWAYMAN]. Please! [*The girls move a little
to the left to avoid him but he follows to listen.*] But you
wrote that he was handsome, gallant and charming?

HARRIET. And so he was until I said that fatal "I do." Then
overnight, he changed from Prince Charming into a dragon.
So very jealous he chained me in my room and fed me only
boiled potatoes. Oh, Sophia, he was the very picture of a
raving, mad Irishman.

HIGHWAYMAN. You have only yourself to blame, madam.
What sensible English girl marries an Irishman?

SOPHIA [*annoyed*]. Our conversation is private, sir. I entreat
you, go on about your business.

HIGHWAYMAN [*grand-angry*]. Oh, very well. Hoity-toity! I'll
look for my pistol. [*Searches as they continue.*]

HARRIET. So, when he'd run through half my fortune, I ran

away. But I have reason to believe he's following me. I hope
to beg the protection of our aunt or of your father.

SOPHIA. My father! My aunt! Oh, no! Sweet Harriet, accom-
pany me to the Inn at Upton and we shall make a better
plan. [*They link arms and go out* D L, *followed by* HONOUR.
HIGHWAYMAN *has by now found his pistol.*]

HIGHWAYMAN [*crying in delight*]. Ahah! Eureka! [*Brandishes
the pistol, turns, runs down to where the girls were.*] Now,
ladies, your money or . . . [*Realizes they are gone and
starts* L *after them.*] Wait! Wait, ladies! I'm ready now!

WESTERN [*from off* R]. Hi, there! You! Young man! One
moment, sir!

[WESTERN *enters* R.]

HIGHWAYMAN [*seeing bigger game, running to* WESTERN].
Your money or your life!

WESTERN [*a great cry*]. Don't threaten me, you blackguard!
I'll set my dogs on you! [HIGHWAYMAN *screams and drops
his pistol.* WESTERN *retrieves it, waves it at* HIGHWAYMAN.]
Have you seen a young gentlewoman pass this way?

HIGHWAYMAN [*near tears*]. I have seen three, my lord.

WESTERN. Which way did they go? [HIGHWAYMAN *points* L.
WESTERN *goes in that direction.* HIGHWAYMAN *follows him.*]

HIGHWAYMAN. Please, sir, my pistol. May I have it? It was
my father's and has a sentimental value.

WESTERN [*screaming*]. Be off with you and learn a trade to
which you are better suited. [*Goes out* L, *carrying the pistol.*
HIGHWAYMAN *retreats, tripping over Tom's staff. He hears
a man whistling off* R *and picks up staff.*]

HIGHWAYMAN [*demoralized*]. Once more . . . I'll try once
more.

[MR. FITZPATRICK, *a large, florid man with a terrible temper
and an Irish accent, enters* R. HIGHWAYMAN, *brandishing the
staff, runs to him and cries:*]

HIGHWAYMAN. Your money or your life!

FITZPATRICK [*enraged*]. Ah, get out of there! [*Grabs the

staff.] Shure, you English are all a lot of cutpurses and thieves. [*Hits* HIGHWAYMAN *with the staff.* HIGHWAYMAN *falls to the ground.* FITZPATRICK *throws the staff away and pulls* HIGHWAYMAN *up by his cape.*]

HIGHWAYMAN. Please, don't hit me, sir. I pray you, go your way in peace.

FITZPATRICK. Faith, stop clackin' the tongue in your worthless head! Are you after seeing a gentlewoman pass by?

HIGHWAYMAN [*thoroughly frightened*]. Ay, good sir. Three of them. And an angry gentleman.

FITZPATRICK. Three, d'ye say, and a man? Shure, she's run off with a fellow that's made her part of an Eastern harem! [*Starts* L, *forgetting to let* HIGHWAYMAN *go and dragging him along.*]

HIGHWAYMAN. Sir . . . good sir . . .

FITZPATRICK. What is it?

HIGHWAYMAN. Would you mind putting me down, sir?

FITZPATRICK. Ah, to the devil with ye! [*Thrusts* HIGHWAYMAN *from him and goes out* D L. HIGHWAYMAN *crumples* C.]

HIGHWAYMAN [*weeping*]. Oh, was ever a man so unlucky! After years of study, to learn I am unsuited to my trade. Perhaps I should have been a constable. I'm better at directing traffic than I am at robbery. [*There is a sound of footsteps at* R. *He is terrified.*] There's someone coming!

MISS WESTERN [*voice, off* R]. You, there! You!

HIGHWAYMAN [*looking off*]. It's a lady! An old lady! She looks terribly fierce! [*Runs and hides behind the tree.*]

[MISS WESTERN *enters* D R.]

MISS WESTERN. Young man! [*Crossing toward the tree.*] Young man, come back here. [*Stumbles on the staff where Fitzpatrick has thrown it, picks it up and crosses to the tree.*] Come out of there, I say!

HIGHWAYMAN [*seeing her with staff, coming out, crying*]. Mercy! Mercy! [*Throws himself, face down, at her feet.*]

MISS WESTERN. Have you seen an angry gentleman on this path?

HIGHWAYMAN. Two! Two angry gentlemen went off toward
Upton . . . most ferocious they were . . . a-chasing some
young woman. One stole my pistol.

MISS WESTERN. Two! Oh, dear me, and chasing a girl! My
brother with a pistol and his ungovernable temper. [*In her
concern she nervously pounds the staff on the ground.*]
Someone will come to harm tonight. Someone will be injured. [*She pounds several times.*]

IIIGHWAYMAN [*frightened out of his wits*]. No, please! No
more. Here! Take my purse! [*Reaches it up to her.*] I've
only got a few shillings but take them, I beg you, and be
on your way!

MISS WESTERN [*surprised*]. Very well . . . if that will give
you pleasure. [*Starts off* D L.] What a very peculiar young
man. [*Goes out* D L. HIGHWAYMAN, *making certain she has
gone, rises.*]

HIGHWAYMAN. Oh, England, to what depths have you fallen,
England? It's not safe for a dishonest man to be out on the
roads alone at night! [*Runs hastily off* U R.]

[PARTRIDGE *enters* D R.]

PARTRIDGE. All right! All right! Get that tree out of there!

[*Two servants rush on, get the tree and rush it off as a third
goes for the moon.*]

PARTRIDGE. Leave the moon, you blockhead! It's still night!
Set up the Inn at Upton!

[*The servants bring in a large table which they set at* L C.
*There are a few stools on it which they remove and place
on the upstage side. There are a quill pen and some paper
on the table. At the same time, one servant places a small
table and stool 'way* U L. *As soon as this is done,* JUSTICE
DOWLING *enters* U L *and sits at this small table.*]

DOWLING [*calling angrily*]. Service! Service! I must have my
dinner at once!

SUSAN [*a pretty young maid at Upton and one of the servants*]. One moment, sir.

DOWLING. I'm a circuit judge and I've a courtroom full of criminals awaiting me at London. I can delay no longer.

SUSAN. I'll be as quick as I can, sir.

PARTRIDGE [*crossing to the large table and displaying it*]. This is the dining room of the Inn at Upton. Pretty, isn't it? [*Proudly modest.*] I designed it myself. And here—[*Walks along the stage to* R.]—these doors lead to the sleeping chambers . . . [*Realizing they aren't there.*] Where are the doors, you dunderheads? [*The servants rush the rolling doors on. One is placed at* C *about halfway up the stage, perpendicular to the footlights. To the right of it, a small table surrounded by two chairs or stools is placed. The other two doors are placed parallel to the footlights at far* R *about a third of the way upstage. A stool is placed behind each. As the servants arrange them,* PARTRIDGE *ad libs the following dialogue, enough to cover.*] Hurry, there! We can't keep all these people waiting! Bestir yourselves, you numbskulls, the gentlemen grow impatient. This was supposed to be done in the twinkling of an eye. [*To audience.*] I' truth, I think it a pretty effect. [*Slightly embarrassed.*] Well, anyway, it will serve. [*Sits on his stool* D R.] The Inn at Upton and its gracious landlady, Mrs. Whitefield.

[MRS. WHITEFIELD, *an elderly innkeeper, enters* U L *and comes down to audience.*]

MRS. WHITEFIELD [*to audience*]. As my late husband used to say, I may put all the good I have ever got by being a landlady in my eye and never see the worse for it.

[SUSAN *enters* U L, *bringing a tray to* DOWLING *who eats, back to the audience, ignoring the rest of the action.*]

MRS. WHITEFIELD. That's my chambermaid, Susan. [SUSAN *comes down to audience and curtsies, smiling.* MRS. WHITEFIELD *sums up her opinion.*] Worthless. [*To* SUSAN.] Get on with your work, hussy!

[SUSAN *dusts the large table.* TOM *and* MRS. WATERS *enter* D L. *Seeing* SUSAN, *he calls.*]

TOM. Hey, there, my girl. We require two chambers and a bite to eat!

SUSAN [*curtsying*]. Come this way, sir. [*Starts* R. *They start to follow but* MRS. WHITEFIELD, *looking at* MRS. WATERS' *dress, stops them.*]

MRS. WHITEFIELD. Hey-day! Where is that beggar wench going? I'll have no gypsies in my house!

MRS. WATERS [*furious*]. Madam! [*To* TOM.] Was ever a gentlewoman so insulted?

TOM [*to* MRS. WHITEFIELD]. This is no gypsy but—[*Placing his hand on his heart.*]—the widow of an officer in his Majesty's Service.

MRS. WHITEFIELD. An officer's widow, eh? She looks as if she came straight from the battlefield.

TOM. Madam has been in an accident and earnestly wishes to purchase a dress if you have one to spare. We will pay well.

MRS. WHITEFIELD [*an instant change of manner*]. Forgive a near-sighted old lady, my lord. I now see you are indeed gentle people. Two chambers, some supper and a dress. The best I have is at your ladyship's service.

MRS. WATERS [*icy*]. You are most kind.

MRS. WHITEFIELD [*smoothly*]. And quite inexpensive. Will your ladyship step up to my chamber? [*Points off* R.]

MRS. WATERS. Willingly. But first, I beg you, is there a surgeon in the neighborhood? This gentleman has been injured in defending me.

MRS. WHITEFIELD. The best surgeon in the kingdom. To watch him draw blood is poetry. Will your ladyship follow me? [*Picks up Tom's pack.*] I'll take your luggage—[*She makes the word an insult.*]—to your room, sir, and send the surgeon. [*Starts* R, *followed by* MRS. WATERS. *As she passes* PARTRIDGE, *she yells:*] Partridge! Your service is required in the dining room! [*The ladies go out* D R.]

PARTRIDGE [*leaping up, to audience*]. See? I told you I'd come into the story. It picks up from here on. [*Picks up a little satchel from behind proscenium and runs* L *to the dining table where* TOM *has seated himself.*] Anyone want a barber?

TOM. Not a barber, a surgeon.

PARTRIDGE. Lud, sir, it's all one! [*Unwraps Tom's bandage, looks at his head, makes a face.*] Ugh!

TOM. What is it?

PARTRIDGE. If you please, sir, I will inspect your head and when I see into your skull I will give my opinion of your case.

TOM. I hope the skull is not fractured.

PARTRIDGE. Fractured? [*Thumps Tom's head a few times.*] I think not. But fractures are not always the most dangerous symptoms. A hot towel, Susan. [SUSAN *goes off* U L.]

TOM. Am I in danger, then?

PARTRIDGE. Ah, surely, who is there among us, in the most perfect health, who can be said not to be in danger?

[SUSAN *returns, hands him towel and then goes out* U L. PARTRIDGE *daubs at Tom's wound.* TOM *screams.* PARTRIDGE *inspects Tom's hair.*]

PARTRIDGE. Your hair wants cutting.

TOM. I prithee, sir, kindly remember which of your trades you practice.

PARTRIDGE [*grandly*]. Surgery is not a trade. It is a profession. [*Takes a bottle from his bag, looks regretfully at the hair.*] Pity . . . [*Pours something from bottle to towel.*] You look as if you have come a good way, sir.

TOM. Aye . . . from Somersetshire.

PARTRIDGE. Somersetshire! [*Daubs at Tom's wound.* TOM *screams.*] There, sir, if it doesn't hurt, it can't be good for you. Do you know a certain Squire Allworthy, sir?

TOM. Why, yes. Till last week I lived within the glow of the Squire's goodness.

PARTRIDGE [*sarcastic*]. Aye, I remember the Squire's goodness. But . . . pardon me, sir, for my inquisitiveness, but . . . can you . . . can you tell me your name?

TOM. My name is Jones.

PARTRIDGE [*collapsing to a chair in shocked surprise*]. Jones!

TOM. Tom Jones.

PARTRIDGE. Tom Jones, the son of Jenny Jones? The ward of Squire Allworthy?

TOM. The very same. But, Mr. Barber or Mr. Surgeon or Mr. Barber-Surgeon, you seem to know me.

PARTRIDGE. Have you ever heard of one Partridge, reputed by many to be the . . . friend . . . of Jenny Jones?

TOM. Indeed I have.

PARTRIDGE [*rising, with dignity*]. I am that Partridge.

TOM [*leaping up in amazement*]. You! Partridge! Father! [*Embraces him.*]

PARTRIDGE [*struggling from the embrace*]. Nay . . . nay . . . sir . . . I prithee, set me free. I have not that great honor. I absolve you from all filial duty; you are no son of mine.

TOM [*releasing him*]. But I have always thought . . .

PARTRIDGE. So many thought the same . . . but I was only a friend to Jenny Jones. I taught her Greek and Latin.

TOM. What need had a serving girl of Greek and Latin?

PARTRIDGE. That's what they all asked.

TOM. But then, who is my father?

PARTRIDGE. Only God or Jenny Jones can answer that. But I have suffered as many cruelties as though I were indeed your father.

TOM. Poor barber-surgeon, I should be very glad if I could make amends to you, but my whole fortune is only what I had with me when Squire Allworthy sent me away. I go now to London to sink into oblivion and forget the dearest, sweetest girl a man ever knew—Miss Sophia Western.

PARTRIDGE. Please, sir, let me attend you in your expedition to London. I want nothing but to leave this place, and to travel with a man such as yourself. It would be an honor to be your servant.

TOM. I have nothing to offer, but you are welcome to share my poverty and I shall be the richer for your company. [*Shakes* PARTRIDGE'S *hand.*]

PARTRIDGE. Oh, thank you, sir. I'll go and fetch my belongings and return. [*Hastily throws his things back into medical kit.*]

TOM. But what about my head? Will you not bandage it?

PARTRIDGE. Oh, no, sir. Let the air get to it. Let the wound breathe. It's nature's way.

[MRS. WHITEFIELD, *followed by* MRS. WATERS, *now neatly dressed, enters* D R. *She leads* MRS. WATERS *to door at* C, *opens it.* MRS. WATERS *goes through it.*]

MRS. WATERS. I am very fatigued and would prefer to sup in my room if that is convenient.

MRS. WHITEFIELD. Susan will fetch you a tray.

MRS. WATERS. And prithee, inquire whether the young gentleman with whom I arrived will join me?

MRS. WHITEFIELD. Your servant, madam. [*Bows and shuts the door.* MRS. WATERS *sits right of table.* MRS. WHITEFIELD *crosses to* TOM.] My lady begs you will attend her at supper. She is in the first room in the passage. [*Crosses to* DOWLING, *who rises and settles his bill with her in pantomime.*]

PARTRIDGE [*poking* TOM *slyly*]. A lady, eh?

TOM [*shrugging it off*]. Just some poor wretch whose life I saved along the road. She seems to have taken a fancy to me. It would be ungentlemanly not to attend her.

PARTRIDGE. Your manners do you credit, sir. Go to her. I'll be back at once. [TOM *crosses into* MRS. WATERS' *room and sits left of table. They pantomime a conversation, quietly, so as not to distract from the rest of the action. Meanwhile,* MRS. WHITEFIELD *takes Dowling's tray out* U L. *As* PARTRIDGE *starts* L, DOWLING *calls him.*]

DOWLING. A moment, sir. [PARTRIDGE *joins him* U L.] Was not that gentleman you were speaking with Mr. Jones, the ward of Squire Allworthy?

PARTRIDGE. He was, sir, but is no more.

DOWLING. Oh?

PARTRIDGE. 'Tis a terrible story, sir . . . [*They turn upstage as* PARTRIDGE *tells the story, and we no longer hear them.*]

[SOPHIA, HARRIET *and* HONOUR *enter* D L.]

HARRIET [*nervously*]. Sophia, it doesn't look very clean.

SOPHIA. Oh, Harriet, we are tired and hungry and though cleanliness is next to godliness, it is next to impossible on the road to London. This will do.

[MRS. WHITEFIELD *enters* U L *and crosses to them.*]

MRS. WHITEFIELD. May I serve you, ladies?

SOPHIA. Have you two rooms?

HARRIET. Two clean rooms?

MRS. WHITEFIELD. Of course. This way, ladies. [*Leads them to doors at* R. *As they go:*]

HARRIET. I am too exhausted to sup, dear cousin. I shall go straight to bed. Good night.

SOPHIA. Good night, Harriet. [HARRIET *enters door at far* R, SOPHIA *and* HONOUR *the one left of it. They close the doors and sit, unseen, behind them.* MRS. WHITEFIELD *crosses* U L *and goes out.* PARTRIDGE *and* DOWLING *turn and walk downstage as* PARTRIDGE *finishes his story.*]

PARTRIDGE [*who's been making it more dramatic*]. . . . and then, Squire Allworthy, who is renowned for his goodness, stripped my innocent master naked, had him beaten, turned the dogs on him and sent him out into the world without a farthing.

DOWLING [*surprised*]. What! Allworthy did that! How surprising! I should speak to Mr. Jones . . .

PARTRIDGE. Oh, not now, sir. He's with a lady.

DOWLING. Yes, well, I haven't time anyway. Your story has made me even later than I was. I have to be in London an hour ago. [*Runs off* D L.]

PARTRIDGE [*calling after him*]. Don't worry, sir, with a good horse you'll make it still. [*Picks up his medical kit and goes out* D L.]

[*At the same time* SUSAN *enters* U L *with a tray containing two plates of rib roast, with bones, knives and forks, two mugs and napkins, which she takes to* MRS. WATERS' *room.*

TOM *and* MRS. WATERS *are by now looking deep into one another's eyes across the table. They draw back as* SUSAN *enters.*]

SUSAN. Your supper, my lady. [*Sets it on the table.* HONOUR *comes out of center door, closing it behind her. She crosses* L, *meeting* SUSAN *coming from Mrs. Waters' room and closing door. They exchange a few words and go off together* U L.]

TOM [*rubbing his hands in delight over the food*]. Ah, most excellent. [*Begins to eat, speaking with mouth full.*] I've had no food since morning.

MRS. WATERS [*is she looking at him or the food*]. It looks very tempting . . .

TOM [*eating like mad, through food*]. But you're not eating . . .

MRS. WATERS [*offering him a languorous glance*]. I could not manage a bite . . . but I prithee, sir, make free . . .

TOM. It's delicious.

MRS. WATERS [*romantically*]. I have a very high opinion of you, sir.

TOM [*eating, eating, eating*]. Thank you, madam.

MRS. WATERS. But why not? After all, you, a total stranger saved me . . . [*He throws down his knife and fork. She, right to his face.*] A defenseless woman. [TOM *looks into her eyes a moment, seems to get the message, then picks up the bone from his plate and begins to gnaw on it.*]

TOM. The laws of chivalry remain, madam.

MRS. WATERS. But how few obey them. [*Gives him another languorous look, sighing rapturously. He throws down the bone and looks at her.*] Is there something you wish to ask me?

TOM [*obviously there is; struggling with himself, then saying*]. No.

MRS. WATERS. Come . . . say what's in your mind . . . don't be shy . . .

TOM [*it's difficult*]. Well, well . . . are you really not hungry?

MRS. WATERS [*disappointed, touching her throat*]. I am full up to here. [*Gives him her plate. He falls to on her food. Sarcastically:*] It's so nice to see a man who eats well. [TOM *puts down knife and fork, lifts his mug and toasts her. She quickly picks up her mug, smiles and clicks it against his. He takes a deep drink, she sips a bit.*] I suppose all that food gives you that strong, muscular figure. [*Puts down her mug.*]

TOM [*eating again*]. A man must eat to keep up his strength.

MRS. WATERS. Indeed. I warrant you are very strong . . . and your face so sympathetic. [TOM *answers but his mouth is full and we can't understand him.*] Why, sir, there is good nature painted in your every glance.

TOM [*throwing down knife and fork*]. Ah . . . I feel much better.

MRS. WATERS [*rising, moving in front of table, looking at his plate, then picking up second bone*]. I believe you've left a bit of meat on this. [*Offers it to him.*] Waste not, want not.

TOM [*rising, too*]. No more, madam. [*She drops the bone, picks up a napkin and delicately wipes her fingers, looking, all the while, at* TOM.] But is there nothing that you wish?

MRS. WATERS. I wish . . . [*Looks at him a long moment, then holds out napkin.*] I wish that you would wipe your fingers. [TOM *takes the napkin and wipes furiously as* MRS. WATERS *moves the door in front of the table parallel to the footlights, blocking them from view.*]

[HONOUR *enters* U L *with tray of food which she carries to Sophia's room. She opens the door and enters.*]

HONOUR [*seen through door, excited*]. Madam! Madam! Who does your ladyship think is in this house?

SOPHIA [*rising from stool, frightened*]. I hope my father has not overtaken us!

HONOUR. No, madam! It is one worth a hundred fathers! Mr. Jones, himself, is here this very moment.

SOPHIA. Mr. Jones! It is impossible! I cannot be so fortunate. Quick! Help me with my hair. [*Shuts the door.*]

[MR. FITZPATRICK *enters* D L.]

FITZPATRICK [*yelling*]. Innkeeper! Ho, Innkeeper!

[MRS. WHITEFIELD *enters* U L.]

MRS. WHITEFIELD. Your pleasure, my lord?

FITZPATRICK. Shure, I'm lookin' for a woman . . .

MRS. WHITEFIELD [*shocked*]. Sir!

FITZPATRICK [*in a rage*]. For me wife! Me wife who I have reason to believe has just sought shelter here with some impudent coxcomb.

MRS. WHITEFIELD. How dreadful for you, sir, but no lady has arrived recently—[*He gives her a coin.*]—unless it is that vile creature in the first room. [*Points toward* MRS. WATERS' *room, and he runs toward it.*]

FITZPATRICK [*yelling, as he goes*]. Wretch! Ingrate! [*Throws open the door, revealing* TOM *and* MRS. WATERS *standing close with hands clasped together.*] Oh, faithless wife! Prepare to meet your Maker. [*Enters the room.*]

MRS. WATERS [*breaking away*]. Help! Murder! Help! Robbery! Help!

TOM [*stepping between her and* FITZPATRICK]. How dare you, sir? This lady is a widow.

FITZPATRICK. Not yet, she isn't, but you'll have to make her so or I'll make myself a widower. [*Tries to reach* MRS. WATERS. TOM *prevents it, grapples with him.* MRS. WATERS *continues to cry "Help!" as* HARRIET *rushes from her room to Sophia's.*]

HARRIET [*screaming over fight noise*]. Cousin, I am terrified. I think I hear my husband's voice! [*Slams Sophia's door as* MRS. WATERS *rushes out of her room.*]

MRS. WATERS. Help, help! I prithee, help!

[SUSAN *enters* U L *and stands behind* MRS. WHITEFIELD *at table* L C, *watching.* TOM, *struggling with* FITZPATRICK, *pushes him upstage, then rushes to* MRS. WATERS.]

TOM. Do you know him?

MRS. WATERS. No! [FITZPATRICK *rushes to them.* TOM *stands between him and* MRS. WATERS.]

FITZPATRICK. Let me at her!

TOM. You blackguard, this is not your wife!

FITZPATRICK. Do you insult me, sir?

TOM. But look at the lady! [*Steps back, displaying* MRS. WATERS.]

FITZPATRICK [*startled*]. Shure, 'tis not me wife at all!

MRS. WATERS. Indeed, sir, you are quite mad!

FITZPATRICK [*still raging*]. Then why were you after masqueradin' as me wife?

MRS. WHITEFIELD [*crossing to them, angrily*]. Come, sirs, this is a respectable house. I will have no brawling!

MRS. WATERS. Respectable! It is a perfect bedlam and you a witch!

MRS. WHITEFIELD. Impudence! To insult me from inside my own dress!

MRS. WATERS. And what will people think of me? In the midst of a tavern brawl? [*Pathetically.*] What has a gentle-woman but her reputation?

TOM [*to* FITZPATRICK]. You will apologize to this lady at once!

FITZPATRICK. Never! You have both insulted me! I demand satisfaction of you, sir, in the morning!

TOM [*angry*]. I'll give it to you now.

FITZPATRICK. I must deny meself the pleasure of killin' you till I have found me wife! I know she's here. [*Rushes off* R.] I'll find her. By my soul, I will!

MRS. WATERS [*to* TOM]. Kind sir, what must you think of me, so continually affronted by strange men.

MRS. WHITEFIELD. He thinks you the very gypsy that you are, madam!

MRS. WATERS. Hag!

TOM [*to* MRS. WHITEFIELD]. Hold your tongue, landlady!
[MRS. WATERS *bursts into tears and rushes to her room.*
TOM *follows to comfort her, shutting the door behind them.*
PARTRIDGE *enters* D L *with a knapsack which he puts on the*
table, then sits. At the same time:]

FITZPATRICK [*voice, off* R]. I know you're in there, you she-
devil! Come out, I say!

WOMAN [*voice, off* R]. Help . . . help . . . murder . . .
thieves . . . help!

MRS. WHITEFIELD [*upset*]. Ah, what further mischief! [*Dashes*
off R, *calling behind her.*] Susan, come help me, you worthless wretch!

[SUSAN *runs across and out at* R *as* SOPHIA *comes out of her*
room, closing the door on the terrified HARRIET *and* HON-
OUR. SOPHIA *crosses* L *to* PARTRIDGE.]

SOPHIA. Excuse me, sir, but do you know if a young man
called Tom Jones is lodged at this inn?

PARTRIDGE. Aye, madam, he is. I have the honor to be his
servant.

SOPHIA [*overjoyed*]. Oh! I prithee conduct me to his chamber
at once.

PARTRIDGE. Impossible, madam, my master is at supper with
a lady.

SOPHIA [*horrified*]. With a lady! Oh, no!

PARTRIDGE. Oh, he is quite an amiable rogue the way all the
women chase after him.

SOPHIA. All the women!

PARTRIDGE. This one . . . and only a few days since he was
obliged to leave Somersetshire where a rich lady of fashion,
Miss Sophia Western, was madly in love with him.

SOPHIA [*shocked*]. Sophia Western! And now another! [*Runs*
back to her room mumbling.] The cad! Oh, perfidious love!
[*Throws open the door.*] He's here!

HARRIET [*terrified*]. My husband!

SOPHIA. Tom Jones!

HONOUR. How happy my lady must be!

SOPHIA. Happy! He is supping with some hussy. He is not only a villain. He is a low, despicable wretch!

HONOUR [*always ready*]. Has my lady thought of marrying Lord Dunwiddy? He has a pretty wit, so they say.

SOPHIA. Never mention another man to me! I am through with all of them!

HARRIET. Was that my husband's voice?

SOPHIA. I forgot to ask. But it doesn't matter. We're leaving at once. Get your things! [HARRIET *rushes to her room as* SOPHIA *cries.*] Oh, Honour! Men would be such perfect beings had God not put women on this earth!

HONOUR [*sensibly*]. Then where'd we be, madam?

[*As* HARRIET *closes her door,* FITZPATRICK *enters* D R, *followed by* MRS. WHITEFIELD *and* SUSAN.]

FITZPATRICK. I swear I'll find her! [*Stops in front of Harriet's door and bangs on it.*] Come out of there!

MRS. WHITEFIELD. I'll have no more of this! [*Grabs one arm, yells:*] Susan! [SUSAN *grabs the other arm.*] Get him to the kitchen! [*They pull him along. As he passes Sophia's door he breaks free and opens it.*]

FITZPATRICK. Are you here then?

HONOUR [*screaming*]. Robbers!

FITZPATRICK [*formally*]. Your servant, ladies. [*Shuts the door, and* MRS. WHITEFIELD *and* SUSAN *pull him* L.]

MRS. WHITEFIELD. Get him a cup of tea, Susan, to calm him down. [*They are now behind the dining table* L C. FITZPATRICK *breaks free of* MRS. WHITEFIELD.]

SUSAN [*still hanging gamely on*]. Your help, Mr. Partridge? [PARTRIDGE *grabs the other arm and helps* SUSAN *drag* FITZPATRICK *off* U L. MRS. WHITEFIELD *stands gasping at the table.* HARRIET, *a handkerchief to her eyes, crying, comes out of her room, and* SOPHIA *comes out of hers. They cross to* MRS. WHITEFIELD.]

MRS. WHITEFIELD. Leaving, ladies, at this hour?

SOPHIA. I find your inn too noisy. Here. [*Hands* MRS. WHITE-FIELD *some coins.*] Is there a coach to London?

MRS. WHITEFIELD. There's one outside, just leaving, that con-
nects at Salisbury. [*Goes out* U L.]

HARRIET [*wiping eyes with handkerchief*]. Do let us leave,
cousin, before we meet Heaven knows whom. [HONOUR
*rushes from the room, carrying the luggage and Sophia's
muff.*]

HONOUR. My lady, you forgot your muff.

SOPHIA. Oh! [*Automatically, she slips it on, then remembering, pulls it off.*] Oh, no! The very muff defiled by that
scoundrel Jones. I never want to see it again. [*Throws it on
the table.*]

HARRIET. I do entreat you, cousin, hurry!

SOPHIA [*seeing pen and paper*]. Wait! [*Takes pen and hastily
scribbles.*] I'll just put my name and Lady Bellaston's address in it. He's bound to see it and then the villain will
know that I know all.

HARRIET. But he'll also know where to find you!

SOPHIA [*slipping the paper in the muff*]. Then I shall have
the pleasure of refusing to see the faithless wretch! Come.
[*Leads* HARRIET, *who has dropped her handkerchief on the
table,* L. HONOUR *follows.*]

HONOUR [*stopping*]. I've just had a thought, madam.

SOPHIA. Yes?

HONOUR [*offering the best solution*]. Sir Frederick Mainwar-
ing!

SOPHIA [*irritated*]. Oh, Honour! [*Sweeps out* D L, *followed
by* HARRIET *and* HONOUR. TOM *comes out of Mrs. Waters'
room.*]

TOM. Good night, madam. I hope this excitement will not dis-
turb your slumbers. [*Closes the door and crosses to the
table, where he sees Sophia's muff.*] Good heavens! [*Picks
it up.*] Sophia's muff! I'd know it anywhere!

[PARTRIDGE *enters* U L.]

TOM. Partridge! This muff! How did it get here?

PARTRIDGE. I don't know . . . but . . . [*Looking at it.*] Let

me see, I saw it upon the arm of the lady who asked for
you.

TOM. Sophia! She's here! She asked for me!

PARTRIDGE. She would have disturbed you if I would have
told her where you were.

TOM. She wanted me and you did not bring her to me! You
fool! You blockhead!

PARTRIDGE [*defending himself*]. I told her you were engaged
with a lady!

TOM. With a lady! Oh, I am undone! Curse you for a villain!
Where is she now?

PARTRIDGE. Upon my life, I know not, sir!

TOM [*calling*]. Landlady! Landlady!

[MRS. WHITEFIELD *hurries in* U L.]

MRS. WHITEFIELD [*entering*]. Sir?

TOM. Have you seen the most beautiful lady in the world?

MRS. WHITEFIELD [*answering carefully*]. Indeed, sir, I saw the
lady you supped with.

TOM. Not her! The one I mean was wearing this muff!

MRS. WHITEFIELD. Oh, that most beautiful lady in the world.
Yes. She and some other ladies just left for London on the
coach.

TOM [*crushed*]. Left . . . for London! [*Slips his hand in the
muff and kisses it.*] Oh, Sophia . . . my only love. . . .
What's this? [*Takes the paper from the muff and reads.*]
"S. Western at Lady Bellaston's, Grosvenor Square." [*To*
PARTRIDGE.] Run, fool, hire horses at once! I'll get my
pack. [PARTRIDGE *runs out* D L. TOM *runs* R.]

MRS. WATERS [*opening her door as* TOM *passes*]. Oh, sir . . .

TOM. I cannot now attend you, madam. I am called away.

MRS. WATERS. What? Would you leave me alone in this den
of madmen?

TOM. I would with pleasure, madam. By dallying in idle conversation with you, I have lost the sainted lady who is all
I love. [*Dashes off* R. *She returns to her room, shutting
door.*]

[FITZPATRICK *enters* U L, *carrying a teacup to the table* L C.]

FITZPATRICK. She must be here. There's not another inn for miles! [*As he sits, he sees the handkerchief.*] What's this? [*Picks it up.*] Her initials. H.F. [*To* MRS. WHITEFIELD.] She is here! Did you see the woman who dropped this handkerchief?

MRS. WHITEFIELD. Indeed, sir, it must have been dropped by one of those two ladies of quality . . .

FITZPATRICK [*beside himself*]. In which room?

MRS. WHITEFIELD. In none, sir. They have just departed on the London coach.

FITZPATRICK [*a cry of rage*]. A curse upon your English transportation system!

[WESTERN *enters* D L *and crosses to* MRS. WHITEFIELD.]

WESTERN. Landlady! Have you seen a young gentlewoman and her servant?

MRS. WHITEFIELD. I' truth, sir, I vow I have seen dozens on this terrible night.

[TOM *runs in at* R, *carrying his pack and Sophia's muff. As he reaches* C, *he is seen by* WESTERN.]

WESTERN. Ah hah! I have you now, you varlet! [*Raises the Highwayman's pistol, which he still holds.*]

MRS. WHITEFIELD. I prithee, sir, no firearms in the house. They must be left in the stable!

WESTERN [*advancing on* TOM *with the pistol*]. Where is my daughter, sir?

TOM. In truth I do not know.

FITZPATRICK [*seeing* TOM *with pack*]. You villain! You're trying to escape without giving me satisfaction!

WESTERN [*seeing Sophia's muff in Tom's hand*]. Her muff! You have her muff! Tell me where she is or I'll beat it out of you.

TOM. Sir, I beg you would be pacified. I have the muff but upon my honor I have not seen your daughter.

FITZPATRICK. He lies! It's not half an hour since I saw him about to embrace her!

WESTERN. Embrace her! I'll have you hung and smoked! Where, sir, I prithee, where's my daughter?

FITZPATRICK [*starting* R]. This way, sir.

[FITZPATRICK *and* WESTERN *cross toward Mrs. Waters' room.* PARTRIDGE *pops in* D L.]

PARTRIDGE. I have the horses, sir.

TOM [*running* D L]. Then let's make haste for London and Sophia. [*They hurry out* D L.]

WESTERN [*throwing open Mrs. Waters' door*]. What, Sophy, you ungrateful wretch. [*Blind with rage, he grabs* MRS. WATERS *and shakes her.*]

MRS. WATERS. Help! Murder! Robbery!

MRS. WHITEFIELD. Oh, not again!

[MISS WESTERN *enters* D L.]

MISS WESTERN. I beg your pardon, madam, but have you seen an angry gentleman?

MRS. WHITEFIELD. Madam, I am an innkeeper, not a directory of missing persons.

WESTERN [*coming out of Mrs. Waters' room*]. That's not my daughter, you imbecile. She's more than twice her age.

FITZPATRICK. Is that the thanks an honest man gets for trying to help?

WESTERN [*looking* L]. Help, indeed! That young scoundrel has escaped.

MRS. WHITEFIELD [*crossing to them*]. Gentlemen, I cannot stand this noise. [MRS. WATERS *comes out of room to watch.*]

FITZPATRICK. I warrant your daughter went to London on the same coach as me wife.

MRS. WHITEFIELD. Follow them, I pray you, and leave me in peace. Take my horses, take my coach, take anything—but take your leave.

FITZPATRICK. At once. We'll catch them!

MRS. WATERS. What! Would you all leave me, after having so distressed me?

FITZPATRICK. An it please you, come ride with us to London.

MRS. WATERS [*delighted*]. Oooh, how gallant. [*Taking his arm.*] It is seven long years, good sir, since I last saw my husband. [*They cross* L *and go out* D L. WESTERN *follows them but is stopped by* MISS WESTERN.]

MISS WESTERN. Brother!

WESTERN. Sister! How came you in this den of thieves?

MISS WESTERN. I was directed here by a nice young man who gave me several shillings. But what are you doing here?

WESTERN. I? [*Waving the pistol.*] I have joined the chase to London. That varlet Jones is the fox, and when I find his lair I will find my daughter. [*Goes out* D L.]

MISS WESTERN. Merciful heavens! Not with a pistol!

[MISS WESTERN *chases after him, running out* D L. MRS. WHITEFIELD, *now standing before the table* L C, *sinks down on it as* SUSAN *enters from* U L.]

MRS. WHITEFIELD. Ah, Susan . . . I am resolved. I shall sell this place to the church and let them use it as a nunnery!

CURTAIN

ACT THREE

SCENE: *The Inn at Upton and the moon have been removed. At* R, *there is a sofa or love seat placed at an angle to the footlights and a chair placed perpendicularly to it. A small table between them holds a bell. At* L *there is a small writing table and chair. A quill and paper on the table. This furniture should be lighter and more delicate and look more citified than the previous country furniture.*]

AT RISE OF CURTAIN: *The servants are* U C *at the cyclorama struggling to set up a cutout of London Bridge, which is giving them some difficulty.* PARTRIDGE *is just entering* R *and coming down toward the audience.*]

PARTRIDGE [*to audience*]. Well, now we are in London. You can tell by the bridge. [*Gestures back to it just as the servants tip it dangerously.*] Oh, excuse me, London Bridge is falling down. [*Runs back, helps to right it and dismisses the servants, who go out.*]

[*As* PARTRIDGE *comes back downstage,* LADY BELLASTON, *a lady of fashion, enters* R.]

PARTRIDGE. We are in Lady Bellaston's drawing room. [*Takes her hand, introducing her to the audience.*] And this is my lady Bellaston herself. She is a lady of fashion.
LADY BELLASTON [*bowing*]. Lud, sir! You do me too much honor.
PARTRIDGE. . . . widowed and quite satisfied with her lot.
LADY BELLASTON [*to audience*]. I have tried marriage once already and I think once is enough for any reasonable woman.

[LADY BELLASTON *seats herself on her sofa and* PARTRIDGE *continues down to the audience. As he speaks,* SOPHIA *and* HARRIET *enter* D L *and cross to* LADY BELLASTON. *All bow to one another and pantomime greetings.*]

PARTRIDGE. Upon arriving in London, Miss Sophia and Mrs. Fitzpatrick immediately waited upon Lady Bellaston, who was their relation. They told her of the perils of their trip— [*The ladies pantomime talking.*]—and my lady Bellaston was properly horrified.

LADY BELLASTON [*commenting, in ladylike horror*]. La!

PARTRIDGE. Miss Western retired at once, exhausted, to her chamber—[SOPHIA *goes out* U R.]—and though Mrs. Fitzpatrick was anxious to retire as well—[HARRIET *makes as if to follow Sophia.*]—she was detained by Lady Bellaston— [LADY BELLASTON *restrains* HARRIET.]—who, under the guise of friendly inquiry, indulged her curiosity. [PARTRIDGE *goes out* D R. LADY BELLASTON *sits on the sofa, again motioning* HARRIET *to the chair, where she sits.*]

LADY BELLASTON. And is it possible that my sweet, innocent cousin Sophia has flown her father's house and risked all to follow this rogue Jones to London?

HARRIET. Indeed, madam, she perishes with love. She cried all night in the coach . . . my shoulder is still quite damp, I pray you, feel it. [*Offers shoulder to* LADY BELLASTON, *who shakes her head.*]

LADY BELLASTON. And still in love though she found him out with another woman?

HARRIET. She has convinced herself of his innocence. She feels his personal grace is such that women force themselves upon him.

LADY BELLASTON [*very intrigued*]. He sounds a disgusting brute! [*Dying to know.*] What is he like?

HARRIET. By her description he has the figure of Hercules, the face of Adonis and is a very Abelard of romantic fancy.

LADY BELLASTON [*fascinated*]. The vulgar oaf! She must be protected from him.

HARRIET [*regretfully*]. Indeed she must. The matter of his questionable birth makes an alliance . . . out of the question.

LADY BELLASTON [*hastily*]. Of course. Of course. [*Hope-*

fully.] But is there any possibility of his seeking her out here?

HARRIET. I fear there is. She left your address in her muff, which she dropped where he was bound to see it.

LADY BELLASTON. How clever she is at intrigue for one so young . . . and from the country, at that. But have no fear, I'll keep him from her. [*They both rise.*] Rest assured, dear Harriet, that Mr. Jones will never get past me.

[HARRIET *bows and goes out* U R *as* NANCY, *Lady Bellaston's maid, enters* D L.]

NANCY. A Mr. Jones is below, madam. He desires to see you.

LADY BELLASTON. What? Already! The villain! My glass, Nancy. [NANCY *takes a small mirror from her pocket, holds it up for* LADY BELLASTON *to check her appearance.*] You may show him in.

[LADY BELLASTON *sits in an elegant pose on the center of the sofa as* NANCY *crosses* D L, *admits* TOM, *then goes out* D L. TOM *bows.*]

LADY BELLASTON. I am Lady Bellaston. My servant said you were Mr.—[*Gropes for the name.*]—Jones?

TOM. Yes, madam.

LADY BELLASTON. And to what, pray, do I owe the honor of this visit?

TOM. I believe, madam, you are related to Miss Sophia Western?

LADY BELLASTON. I am. What business do you have with her?

TOM [*startled*]. Why . . . why . . . [*Thinking up an excuse.*] While staying last night at the Inn at Upton, I found a muff with the young lady's name and your address in it. I had hoped to return it to her.

LADY BELLASTON. You may leave it with me.

TOM. Unfortunately, I have left it at my lodgings. If my lady could tell me where to find Miss Western, I should be happy to deliver it.

LADY BELLASTON. Come, Mr. Jones, I think you are lying?

TOM. Lying, madam?

LADY BELLASTON. Don't be embarrassed. I personally believe there is a great deal too much truth told. To lie is not only excusable, but commendable. Especially—[*Underlining it.*] —in the case of lovers.

TOM [*trapped*]. Lovers, madam?

LADY BELLASTON. But country people should not lie in the town, Mr. Jones. They are simply no match for the competition. In a word, sir, I know all about you and Miss Western.

TOM. And is she here, then?

LADY BELLASTON. No. Nor shall I tell you where she is. She is resolved not to see you and I have too great a regard for my cousin to assist in carrying on an affair between you two which must end in her ruin as well as your own.

TOM. Alas, madam, I do not wish her ruin. I love her and would sacrifice everything to the possession of my Sophia but Sophia herself.

LADY BELLASTON. Well spoken, Mr. Jones. You may sit down. [*Moves to the left of the sofa making it obvious he should sit by her, which he does.*] I now believe your pretensions to Sophia are not so much presumptuous as imprudent. I love ambition in a young man—[*Looking closely into his face.*] —and I think a man as handsome as yourself could succeed with those who are infinitely superior in fortune.

TOM [*not knowing how to react to this, nervously*]. You . . . flatter me . . . madam.

LADY BELLASTON. Do you mind my saying, Mr. Jones, that your clothes, though doubtless suitable in the country, are not those of a gentleman in the town?

TOM. They are all I have, my lady.

LADY BELLASTON. How unfortunate. I can, perhaps, be of some help. [*Rings the bell on the table.*] My late husband had a large and handsome wardrobe which I think would do for you . . .

TOM. I could not accept . . .

LADY BELLASTON. I insist. I am known for my charitable

work among handsome young men. Besides, the clothes are of no further conceivable use to my late husband.

TOM. But . . .

LADY BELLASTON. And I can't possibly have you visiting here dressed as a stable boy. And I know you will want to return . . . if only to bring Miss Western's muff.

TOM [*politely*]. And to give myself the pleasure of conversing with you again, madam.

[NANCY *enters* D L *and curtsies.*]

LADY BELLASTON. Nancy, show Mr. Jones my Lord Bellaston's wardrobe and allow him to take what he fancies. [NANCY *crosses* U R.] I beg of you to wait upon me this evening at seven. You are a diamond in the rough, Mr. Jones, and I fancy you'll polish up quickly. [TOM *bows and follows* NANCY *out* U R.] Charming. He is everything they said he was. It would be sinful to waste him on Sophia. She's too young to appreciate him. I shall send her to the theatre this evening. [*Goes out* U L.]

[PARTRIDGE *enters* D R, *carrying Sophia's muff.*]

PARTRIDGE. It shows again. You can't leave a country boy alone in the city. And you can surely see, gentle audience, that it was Mr. Jones' innocence this woman played on. He is not a cad. Indeed the opposite. It's in his code of honor to play the gallant to the ladies when they seem to expect it . . . and Lady Bellaston expected it, although the lady, to the eyes of all except herself, is surely past the age of gallantry. But alas, Mr. Jones needs help.

TOM [*off* R]. Partridge, I need help!

PARTRIDGE [*putting muff on stool*]. Yes, sir. Right here, sir.

[TOM *enters* D R. *He has changed to very elegant trousers. Since this is a very quick change he should under-dress them during the intermission. His shirt may remain the same, and he is pulling on a waistcoat as he enters, carrying his coat, a wig and a sword.* PARTRIDGE *helps him into his clothes as they talk.*]

PARTRIDGE. Are you sure going to Lady Bellaston's is wise, sir?

TOM. I must go, Partridge. She is my only clue to the where-abouts of my sweet Sophia. Sophia! Her virtues, her purity, her suffering on my account fill all my thoughts and make commerce with Lady Bellaston even more odious. Yes, I must go. [*He is by now dressed.*] There! Am I all right?

PARTRIDGE [*buckling on sword*]. Excellent, sir.

TOM. Then I am off . . . [*Starts upstage.*]

PARTRIDGE. You forgot the muff, sir. [*Hands it to* TOM *and then goes out* D R. TOM *crosses to sofa.*]

[NANCY *enters* U R.]

NANCY. My lady Bellaston will be detained, sir, and begs you wait. [TOM *nods,* NANCY *curtsies and goes out* U R. TOM *sits on the sofa, putting down the muff.*]

[SOPHIA *enters* D L *and sees* TOM.]

SOPHIA. Oh! What are you doing here?

TOM [*rising, astounded*]. Sophia!

SOPHIA [*suspicious*]. I did not know you were acquainted with Lady Bellaston.

TOM [*lying blatantly*]. I only knew her name—[*Picks up the muff and crosses to her.*]—which I read in your muff. [*Gives it to her.*]

SOPHIA [*nonchalantly*]. Oh, you found it. [*Lying in her turn.*] I wondered where I dropped it. [*Changing the subject.*] But by your clothing, Mr. Jones, you seem to have turned into a gentleman of fashion. I wonder how you managed that so quickly.

TOM [*changing this subject*]. Let us not, I beseech you, waste one of these precious moments in discussing clothing after this long and terrible pursuit.

SOPHIA [*cool*]. Pursuit? Of whom?

TOM. Need I say, of you? Allow me, on my knees—[*Kneels.*] —to beg your pardon.

SOPHIA [*sarcastically*]. My pardon? Why should you ask my

pardon? Just because I heard my name bandied about in a vulgar tavern . . . and you supping with strange women.

TOM. Oh, my only love—[*Rises.*]—do me the justice to think I was never unfaithful to you. Though I despaired of ever seeing you again, I loved you.

SOPHIA. And that woman?

TOM. A mere companion for dinner to whom I spoke of nothing but my love for my Sophia.

SOPHIA [*melting*]. Oh, Tom . . . [*Allows him to embrace her.*]

TOM. And of my hopes . . . to marry her.

SOPHIA. Marry you! Oh, Tom, I dare not even be seen with you. No one . . . not even Lady Bellaston . . . can be trusted not to tell my father, and should he hear, it would bring ruin on us both.

TOM. Ruin! No, I cannot act so base a part. Dearest Sophia, whatever it costs me, I shall renounce you. [*Kisses her.*] I will give you up. [*Kisses her again.*] My love I shall ever retain but from the distance of some foreign land where my voice, my sighs, my despairs, shall never reach your ears. [*Kisses her again.*]

[LADY BELLASTON *enters* D L.]

LADY BELLASTON [*sarcastically*]. I thought, Miss Western, you had been at the play. [TOM *and* SOPHIA *jump apart.*]

SOPHIA. I . . . I . . . left early. I thought it vulgar. It was called *Hamlet.*

LADY BELLASTON. I should not have broken in upon you, Miss Western, had I known you had . . . company.

SOPHIA. No, madam, our business was at an end. Surely you remember, I have often mentioned the loss of my muff, which—[*Not wanting to say who he is.*]—this strange gentleman having found was so kind as to return to me.

LADY BELLASTON [*sarcastically*]. What good fortune. But how could you know, strange gentleman, it was Miss Western's or where to find her in London?

TOM. Her name and your address were written in it.

LADY BELLASTON [*to* SOPHIA]. How clever of you to insure
that all your . . . possessions . . . can return to you.

TOM. It was the luckiest chance imaginable.

SOPHIA. Thank you so much, sir. The muff has great sentimental value to me.

TOM. I believe, madam, it is customary to give some reward
on these occasions. I request no more than the honor of
being permitted to pay another visit here.

LADY BELLASTON. I make no doubt you are a gentleman . . .
by your clothes . . . which are strangely familiar . . . and
my doors are never shut to people of fashion.

TOM. Your servant, ladies. [*Bows and goes out* D L.]

LADY BELLASTON. Upon my word, a pretty young fellow. I
wonder who he is.

SOPHIA. I wonder.

LADY BELLASTON [*laughing*]. I vow you must forgive me,
Sophia, but when I first came into the room, I suspected it
was Mr. Jones himself.

SOPHIA [*trying to pass it off, laughing*]. Did your ladyship,
indeed?

LADY BELLASTON. I can't think what put it into my head as
he was genteelly dressed, which I think is not commonly the
case with your friend.

SOPHIA [*beginning to be upset*]. I beg your ladyship not to
tease me about Mr. Jones.

LADY BELLASTON. Why, Sophy, I shall begin to fear you are
still in love with the man.

SOPHIA. Upon my honor, I am as indifferent to Mr. Jones as
to that strange gentleman who just left us.

LADY BELLASTON. Upon my honor, I believe that.

SOPHIA [*upset, afraid of being revealed*]. Your ladyship's pardon, but I would retire to my chamber.

LADY BELLASTON. No doubt you are weary after your evening
at the play. [SOPHIA *goes out* U R. LADY BELLASTON *crosses
to the table* R *and rings bell. To herself:*] That girl must be
got out of the way. [*Goes to the table* L, *takes up the pen
and begins to write.*]

[HARRIET *enters* U R.]

HARRIET. Pray what is the matter with Sophia? She seems distraught.

LADY BELLASTON [*while writing*]. That bounder Jones has been here.

HARRIET. Jones! Here!

LADY BELLASTON. Though she pretended it was not he, I saw through her little fiction.

[NANCY *enters* U R.]

NANCY. You rang, madam?

LADY BELLASTON. Do you know the house of Miss Western in Jermyn Street?

NANCY. Yes, madam.

LADY BELLASTON. I desire that you should take her this. [*Hands* NANCY *the note.* NANCY *goes out* D L.] I have written Miss Western the whereabouts of her niece. I can no longer be responsible for her safety. The gentleman is too handsome to be trusted.

HARRIET [*shocked*]. You have betrayed Sophia!

LADY BELLASTON [*outraged*]. And would you call this betrayal?

[*The two ladies freeze as* PARTRIDGE *enters* D R.]

PARTRIDGE. Indeed I would. She doesn't care a farthing for Miss Sophia's safety. Her only interest is in my unfortunate master. Oh, she's at a dangerous age, she is. Too old for riding and too young for petit point. Well, hardly had the note been dispatched but Mr. Western was at Lady Bellaston's.

[WESTERN, *furious, storms in* D L, *followed by* MISS WESTERN. LADY BELLASTON *and* HARRIET *unfreeze.*]

WESTERN. Where's my daughter? Where is she? 'Sblood, I'll unkennel her this instant! Show me her chamber!

LADY BELLASTON [*pointing* U R]. The second door to the right.

WESTERN [*charging off* U R]. Daughter! Daughter! I demand instant obedience.

MISS WESTERN [*following him*]. Brother, I beg you mitigate your wrath. [*Remembering her manners, she turns, bows to the others and says:*] So nice to see you, ladies. [*She then runs off* U R.]

HARRIET. But why this sudden change? You were willing to protect her from her father before.

LADY BELLASTON. I acted rashly. It is not for me to come between a parent and a child.

[WESTERN *enters, dragging* SOPHIA *behind him.* MISS WESTERN *follows.*]

WESTERN. There, my lady cousin, stands the most undutiful, defiant child in the world!

LADY BELLASTON [*hypocritically*]. Sophia, listen to a woman old enough to be your—[*Suddenly changing the phrase.*]—your older sister. Heed your father. Obedience to a parent is one of the true joys of life.

SOPHIA [*outraged*]. Spy!

WESTERN. Allworthy and Blifil have come to London. I have sent word to them to meet us at your aunt's.

SOPHIA. I won't see him.

WESTERN. I say you will, and you will.

SOPHIA [*stamping her feet in a frenzy*]. Never, never, never!

MISS WESTERN. Brother, I protest. A woman must be led, not whipped.

WESTERN. That's not women! That's donkeys! [*Drags* SOPHIA *out* D L, *followed by* MISS WESTERN, *who stops just before going out, remembering her manners, half bows and says:*]

MISS WESTERN. A charming visit. [*Giving up in the middle of her curtsy she throws up her hands and follows the others out* D L.]

HARRIET [*having figured it out*]. Lady Bellaston, upon my word. You want Jones for yourself!

LADY BELLASTON. My dear cousin, you are still using my home as a refuge from your husband and, if you wish to remain,

I urge you, say no more. [*Goes out* U R, *followed by* HARRIET.]

[TOM *and* PARTRIDGE *enter* D R.]

TOM. Partridge, I know not what to do. I have had three letters from my Lady Bellaston in as many hours, entreating me to wait upon her.

PARTRIDGE. Oh, sir, that's very serious from a woman of her reputation.

TOM [*regretfully*]. Why won't women leave me alone? Oh, Partridge, beauty like mine is a curse.

PARTRIDGE. I pity you, sir.

TOM. I dare not be uncivil to Lady Bellaston, for then she would deny me entry to her house—and how would I then see my Sophia? And yet, should I attend her and my Sophia hears of it, she may think me unfaithful to her.

PARTRIDGE. It is a pretty pickle. [*Thinks a moment.*] I have it, sir. Propose marriage to Lady Bellaston.

TOM [*shocked*]. Marriage! Are you mad?

PARTRIDGE. No, sir. If you attend Lady Bellaston as a friend, she will find you charming and you'll never get rid of her. But if you propose marriage, she will think you a fortune hunter and you will be free of her.

TOM. Amazing! Most excellent, Partridge, I think you're right. I'll write to her at once. [*They go out* D R.]

[NANCY *immediately enters* D L, *carrying a note.* LADY BELLASTON *appears* U R *and crosses to* NANCY.]

NANCY. A message from Mr. Jones, madam.

LADY BELLASTON [*taking it, delighted*]. Mr. Jones! [*Reads it hastily, utters an angry cry.*] Marriage! He is an unmitigated villain! Take this at once to Miss Western from me and tell her to make the best use of it. [*Hands the note back to* NANCY.] And should Mr. Jones present himself, I am not at home . . . ever! [*Sails out* U R.]

[*A servant pushes a door on* D L *parallel to the footlights and*

exits. NANCY *walks through it and crosses* R. TOM *enters*
D R, *walks* L, *meeting* NANCY *at* C.]

TOM. Is your mistress at home?

NANCY [*haughtily*]. Not to you, sir.

TOM [*delighted*]. Hey day! It worked! That clever Partridge
must be rewarded. [*To* NANCY.] And Miss Sophia, is she
at home?

NANCY. Miss Sophia is gone, sir.

TOM [*horrified*]. Gone? Gone where?

NANCY. I'm sure I don't know, sir. [*Goes out* D R.]

[HARRIET *enters* U R *and crosses to door* D L.]

TOM. Oh! I am ruined! A pox on Partridge!

HARRIET [*opening door and calling through it*]. Sir! . . .
Sir!

TOM [*crossing to her*]. I, madam?

HARRIET. You are Mr. Jones, I believe?

TOM. I have that misfortune.

HARRIET. I dare not linger. I must not be seen. Sophia has
been spirited away.

TOM. Indeed, madam, I know. But where?

HARRIET. She is being held at her aunt's house in Jermyn
Street.

TOM [*happy*]. Oh, thank you, madam. All is not lost. I can
find her again. Blessings on you for a saint. [*Kisses her
hand.*]

HARRIET [*snatching back her hand*]. I must not be seen speaking with you. [*Goes inside, closes the door and goes off*
U L.]

[FITZPATRICK *enters* D R, *catching sight of the disappearing*
HARRIET.]

FITZPATRICK [*calling* TOM]. You, there! You, sir! Who was
that lady you were speaking with?

TOM. In truth, sir, I know not . . . [*Recognizing* FITZPAT-
RICK.] Why, sir, I think we know each other.

FITZPATRICK [*now recognizing him*]. Ah! From Upton! You are Mr. Jones!

TOM. I am.

FITZPATRICK. What a fortunate meeting.

TOM. Indeed, sir, I am glad you have forgiven me that foolish quarrel.

FITZPATRICK [*falsely jolly*]. Our quarrel is forgotten. The fact that you insulted me means nothing. I have today a far better reason—[*Draws his sword.*]—for killing you!

TOM [*moving back, drawing his sword to be ready*]. But why, sir?

FITZPATRICK [*in a rage*]. That lady with whom you have just had a rendezvous . . .

TOM. Yes?

FITZPATRICK. That was no lady . . .

[PARTRIDGE *appears* D R.]

PARTRIDGE [*to audience*]. You won't believe this!

FITZPATRICK. That was my wife! [*Lunges at* TOM.]

[*As many extras as possible rush on at the prospect of a duel crying: "A fight!" "A duel!" "What's all that row?" "Oh, come and watch, Mother, someone may get killed!"* NANCY *is among the crowd. If the actors are equipped to fence, they do. If not,* FITZPATRICK *chases* TOM *around the stage until finally the extras cover the two men and* TOM *lunges at* FITZPATRICK. *If they duel in sight of the audience, the climax of the duel is* TOM'S *getting* FITZPATRICK. *The extras yell throughout.* PARTRIDGE, *too, observes. When* TOM *has lunged, there is a scream from* FITZPATRICK. *Comments from the crowd: "He's got him!" "That does it!" "You owe me a shilling, Bert!" If the two men have been covered, the crowd now breaks, revealing them.*]

FITZPATRICK [*tottering*]. I have satisfaction enough! I am a dead man!

TOM. I hope not . . . but remember, you started it! [FITZPATRICK *crumples to the ground.*]

NANCY. He's killed him! Help! Constable! Murder!

[*A* CONSTABLE *rushes on from* L, *to* TOM *standing over* FITZ-PATRICK.]

CONSTABLE [*grabbing* TOM]. You've killed him.

CROWD [*ignoring* FITZPATRICK]. "Murderer!" "To prison with him!" "He'll hang for this!"

TOM. Will someone at least take care of the gentleman?

NANCY. You've taken care of him! I doubt he has an hour to live! As for you, sir, I give you a week before they hang you.

CONSTABLE [*to the crowd*]. Take him to a surgeon . . . or an undertaker. [*The crowd takes* FITZPATRICK *off* R *and the* CONSTABLE *starts* TOM *off* L.] And as for you, sir, the New-gate Prison.

TOM [*sadly*]. Oh, I am a happy man. I came to London to sink to the depths . . . and I've made it! [*They go out* L.]

[PARTRIDGE *is alone on stage. The servants enter as he talks and clear the door and Lady Bellaston's furniture.*]

PARTRIDGE [*to audience*]. Oh, it was terrible. My innocent master attacked by that wild, jealous Irishman. And surely you, who have seen it all, know my master was not even acquainted with Mrs. Fitzpatrick, who, herself, acted from the kindest motives.

[HONOUR *enters* D R *carrying a note. She goes to* PARTRIDGE.]

HONOUR. Are you Mr. Jones' servant?

PARTRIDGE. Aye, but you'll have to wait. Can't you see I'm busy? [*To audience.*] I followed my master to the jail . . . a terrible place . . . crowded with ruffians and villains . . . and my gentle master . . . not even a private dungeon. [*He is too moved to go on.*]

HONOUR. If you please, sir, I have a message for Mr. Jones.

PARTRIDGE [*testily*]. In a moment! [*To audience.*] I left him to go to the tavern where they took Mr. Fitzpatrick. The Doctor says . . . he's . . . he's dying.

HONOUR. What a talkative rogue you are! You may take the message or not as you choose! It is for your master, from Miss Sophia. [*Presses the note into his hand and goes out* R.]

PARTRIDGE. A note from Miss Sophia! Perhaps that will lift his spirits!

[*By now the furniture is cleared.* TOM *enters* L, *guarded by the* CONSTABLE. *He stands at* L C *and* PARTRIDGE *crosses to him.*]

PARTRIDGE. I have something for you, sir. [*Starts to hand* TOM *the note.*]

CONSTABLE. Here, you can't give the prisoner anything.

PARTRIDGE [*showing note to* CONSTABLE]. It's just a message.

CONSTABLE. It might contain a concealed weapon. [PARTRIDGE *looks quizzically at the tiny note.*]

TOM. May he be allowed to read it to me?

CONSTABLE [*suspicious*]. From a distance.

PARTRIDGE [*breaking the seal*]. It's from Miss Sophia!

TOM. Oh, my gentle Sophia! How sweet . . . how thoughtful . . . a note to bring me courage in my hour of despair.

PARTRIDGE [*reading*]. "Sir, my aunt has just shown me a letter from you to Lady Bellaston which contains a proposal of marriage. This indeed proves the constancy of your love for me. All I now desire is that your name may never more be mentioned to Sophia Western."

TOM [*a cry of pain*]. Ohhh, Partridge, you confounded blackguard! You and your proposal of marriage!

PARTRIDGE [*embarrassed*]. We . . . we all make mistakes, sir.

TOM [*taking a message from his pocket*]. Take her this, you numbskull. She is at Miss Western's in Jermyn Street.

PARTRIDGE. Yes, sir. [*Takes note. The* CONSTABLE *starts* TOM *out* L.]

TOM [*as they go*]. Tell her I love her . . . and I'll be here if there's an answer. [*Half turns away.*] I'll also be here if there isn't. [CONSTABLE *and* TOM *go out* L.]

[*A servant pushes on a door* D R *and exits. At the same time* PARTRIDGE *starts walking* R. BLIFIL *enters* D R, *meeting* PARTRIDGE *in front of the door.*]

PARTRIDGE. Your pardon, sir, is this Miss Western's house?

BLIFIL. Yes. I'm just going there.

PARTRIDGE. Oh, sir, I am not welcome in this house. I entreat you, would you take this letter to Miss Sophia? It is from her lover, Mr. Jones.

BLIFIL. Jones, eh?

PARTRIDGE. They have had a bit of a lover's spat, sir . . . a misunderstanding . . . my fault entirely . . . and this will perhaps clear it up.

BLIFIL [*smiling wickedly, taking note*]. I shall be happy to take care of it. But where, pray, is Mr. Jones, should there be some answer?

PARTRIDGE. In Newgate Prison, sir. A most unhappy event. He was set upon by an Irish madman. They fought and now this Mr. Fitzpatrick, his assailant, is dying. My master's sure to hang! So you can see the importance of this message.

BLIFIL. Oh, indeed. And where is the unfortunate Mr. Fitzpatrick?

PARTRIDGE. With the doctor, sir—no good will it do him— in the inn just two streets down.

BLIFIL. Thank you, my good man. I'll see the message is delivered.

PARTRIDGE. Thank you, sir. [*Turns and goes out* L.]

[WESTERN *enters* R *and comes through the door to* BLIFIL.]

WESTERN. Ah, son-in-law, you are come in good time. We'll have her persuaded to you today.

BLIFIL. My uncle will be here at once, sir . . . but you must excuse me, I have some further business before I can give myself the pleasure of your company. But, sir, have you heard the news?

WESTERN. News? What news?

BLIFIL. Jones has murdered a man.

WESTERN [*delighted*]. What's that? Murder? Is there any hope of seeing him hanged?

BLIFIL. The best hope.

WESTERN [*singing gaily*]. Tol de rol . . . tol de rol . . . I never heard better news in my life. If this fellow be but hanged out of the way, what further trouble can we have of Sophy? [*Sings again, capering around.*] Sing hey nonny nonny fol de rol day!

BLIFIL. I'll attend you presently. [*Goes out* L.]

[*A servant pushes the door out* R. SOPHIA *enters* U R *carrying a large purse, followed by* MISS WESTERN.]

WESTERN [*joyously*]. Ah, there's my girl! As pretty as a picture this enchanted day.

MISS WESTERN. Brother, what means this reversal of attitude? I have not seen you so happy since the day your poor wife died.

WESTERN. What would you say, Sophy, did I give you leave to marry Jones?

MISS WESTERN. Marry Jones!

WESTERN. An he refuse you . . . or be not able to marry you . . . would you then obediently marry Blifil?

SOPHIA. I'll never marry anyone.

WESTERN. What, not Jones?

SOPHIA. Not any man.

WESTERN. A humor you will soon pass out of. So come, my sweet Sophy, if you want not to marry any, surely you will give me your word if Jones won't marry you . . . and you do wed . . . to marry my choice. Come, this is an important matter to me.

SOPHIA. And an indifferent one to me since my aunt disclosed Mr. Jones' perfidy. Very well . . . if you like . . . I will agree.

WESTERN [*singing again*]. Tol de rol . . . tol de rol . . .

MISS WESTERN. I cannot guess what's happened.

[ALLWORTHY *enters* D R.]

WESTERN. Come, neighbor Allworthy . . . all's settled . . .
my Sophy has been won by your nephew.

ALLWORTHY. Mr. Western, while I long to see our families
united, I cannot consent to a marriage against the young
lady's will.

WESTERN. She has agreed. If Jones won't marry her, she'll
marry Blifil.

SOPHIA. If I marry at all.

ALLWORTHY. Why? Why this change?

[BLIFIL *enters* L *and crosses to them.*]

WESTERN. Ah, son-in-law, for so in truth I will soon call you
. . . if all has gone well . . .

ALLWORTHY. What does this mean?

BLIFIL. The trial is to begin within the hour.

ALLWORTHY. Trial? Whose trial?

BLIFIL. Jones has murdered a Mr. Fitzpatrick. He will surely
hang!

SOPHIA [*shocked*]. Tom! A murderer! So that's why . . .

MISS WESTERN. Fitzpatrick? Can that be our cousin Harriet's
husband? If so, Mr. Jones is indeed unlucky for our family.

ALLWORTHY. I'll not believe it. He is a rogue, I grant you,
but not a murderer!

BLIFIL. Come, let us go to the trial. He shan't escape his fate.
I promise you that.

[*The servants run on, bringing a judge's bench. If possible a
high, traditional bench; if that is too cumbersome, a long
table will do. They place it* U C, *a chair behind it. They
then arrange themselves as audience to the trial. The Western group stays where it is at* R. HONOUR *joins them.* LADY
BELLASTON, HARRIET *and* NANCY *enter* L, *followed by* PAR-
TRIDGE. *They join the audience. All other available extras
should be used, too. When the court audience is set, the*
CONSTABLE *leads* TOM *in from* U L, *placing him* U L C. *The
audience reacts with a buzz.*]

CONSTABLE [*announcing*]. His Honor, Justice Dowling.

[DOWLING *enters from* U L, *dressed in robes and wig of an English judge. He sits at the Judge's bench.*]

DOWLING. All right . . . all right. Let's get on with this trial. I haven't much time, there's another murderer waiting outside.

CONSTABLE. This man, Tom Jones, stands accused of murdering one Mr. Fitzpatrick.

DOWLING. Murdered Fitzpatrick, eh? Very well. [*Bangs his gavel.*] I rule he shall hang at sundown. Next case!

PARTRIDGE. But, your Honor, it was not murder!

DOWLING. Here, here, quiet! I will have no disrespect for the dignity of this court. [*To* CONSTABLE.] Get 'em all out of here and bring in the next batch.

PARTRIDGE. But, sir, don't you want to hear any witnesses?

DOWLING. If you insist, but it always takes so much time. What witnesses are there?

PARTRIDGE. I, sir. I saw the whole thing. Fitzpatrick fell upon Mr. Jones with no warning. My master only defended himself.

NANCY. That's not true. I was returning to my Lady Bellaston's and I saw this villain Jones set upon that poor man with no provocation and run him through.

DOWLING. Oh, yes . . . well . . . I have heard the evidence and I now rule Tom Jones shall hang at sundown.

PARTRIDGE. Not fair! Not fair!

ALLWORTHY. Of course, it's fair! If he killed the man he must be punished.

DOWLING [*looking at him*]. Aren't you Squire Allworthy of Somersetshire?

ALLWORTHY. Yes.

DOWLING. I thought so. The last time I saw you, you were sick.

ALLWORTHY. My doctor says I must have rest.

DOWLING. Well, why do you want this boy to hang? I should think you'd want to hush the whole thing up.

ALLWORTHY. Sir, you impugn my honor. It is well known that
I respect the law and that I hold a grudge.

DOWLING. Well, if you don't care, I don't care. Hanged at
sundown. Get them all out of here and bring in the next
case.

[MRS. WATERS *enters* L.]

MRS. WATERS. Wait!

DOWLING. What now? What now?

MRS. WATERS [*crossing to him*]. I have evidence in this case.
Material evidence.

DOWLING [*impatient*]. Delays . . . delays!

TOM [*to* PARTRIDGE, *who is near him*]. Upon my word, that's
Mrs. Waters!

PARTRIDGE [*dumbstruck*]. You . . . you know that woman?

TOM. She is the lady with whom I supped at Upton.

PARTRIDGE. Dear Heaven . . . don't you know who she is?
She is . . .

ALLWORTHY [*leaping up, having recognized her*]. You are
Jenny Jones!

MRS. WATERS. I was. I am Mrs. Waters.

TOM. You! Jenny Jones! *Mother!* [*Leaps to embrace her. As*
MRS. WATERS *struggles to escape his embrace, pandemonium
breaks out in the court at this revelation.* DOWLING *pounds
his gavel.*]

DOWLING. Order! Order! Is this a murder trial or a family
reunion?

MRS. WATERS. Neither, sir. He has not committed murder and
I am not his mother. [*Extricates herself from Tom's embrace.*]

TOM [*disappointed*]. Not my mother . . .

MRS. WATERS [*moving to* ALLWORTHY]. You will remember,
sir, I told you long ago you would one day know this child's
true parents. Do you remember twenty-odd winters ago a
man called Summer who visited your home?

ALLWORTHY. Winter . . . summer . . . yes, I do. I disliked

him and was not sorry when he was killed by a runaway horse.

MRS. WATERS. Indeed, sir, but your sister, Miss Bridget, was, I may say, overly fond of him. Just before his fatal accident, they were secretly married. [*A stir of excitement from the crowd.*]

ALLWORTHY. Why did she never tell me?

MRS. WATERS. Knowing your displeasure with the man and your reputation for goodness, she was afraid to tell you. Shortly after his death, she found herself with child. You, at this time, were providently called to London and Miss Bridget engaged me to attend her at the birth of the baby. I took the baby to my mother's house and upon your return, at her request, placed the baby in your bedchamber.

ALLWORTHY. Then he is indeed my nephew?

MRS. WATERS. And technically speaking, not a foundling at all.

ALLWORTHY [*crossing to* TOM]. My boy! [*Embraces* TOM.]

SOPHIA. Not a foundling!

MISS WESTERN [*adjusting her views*]. An excellent match, I've always said.

MRS. WATERS [*to* ALLWORTHY]. I should have told you long ago but only today did I realize how necessary it was when you sent your emissary to me.

ALLWORTHY. Emissary? I sent no emissary!

MRS. WATERS. He said he came from you. This gentleman came to the inn at which I am lodged and mistook me for Mrs. Fitzpatrick—I cannot imagine why, as the gentleman and I had only a nodding acquaintance and but happened to be staying in the same inn. He told me Mr. Jones had murdered my husband. He said that you, sir, would assist me with any money I needed to carry on a prosecution against Jones.

DOWLING. But why should he want to hang his nephew?

ALLWORTHY. I didn't know it was my nephew . . . nor did I send anyone to you, madam. What did this man look like?

MRS. WATERS [*pointing at* BLIFIL]. It was he! [*Sensation in the court.*]

BLIFIL. I never saw that woman in my life!

WESTERN. What, villain, you would hang your own cousin?

ALLWORTHY. I protest, sir, he did not know Tom was his cousin.

DOWLING. But he did! It was in the message that I brought you myself from Mme. Blifil when she lay dying in Salisbury. They were her last words. She said, "Tell my brother— [*Coughs twice as Mrs. Blifil did.*]—Tom Jones is my son."

ALLWORTHY. How came you, sir, not to deliver the message?

DOWLING. Your worship must remember that you were at the time ill in bed and, being in a violent hurry, as indeed I always am, I delivered the message to Mr. Blifil, who swore that he would give it to you.

ALLWORTHY [*crossing to* BLIFIL, *who is* D R]. Villain! You have concealed this fact! [*The court murmurs in shock, those near* BLIFIL *drawing away.*]

BLIFIL. I . . . I . . . I had no such intention, Uncle . . . it . . . it . . . it somehow slipped my mind.

ALLWORTHY. Quit my sight, you blackguard! And let me never hear your name again.

BLIFIL. But . . . but . . . [ALLWORTHY *turns his back on him.* BLIFIL *slowly goes out* R. *The court hisses him.*]

DOWLING. But there is still the question of the murder for which I have already passed sentence.

ALLWORTHY. Oh, can't we hush that whole thing up? The boy's my nephew.

DOWLING. If you'd come to me earlier . . .

MRS. WATERS. My lord, have you seen the corpse?

DOWLING. No . . . no . . . that's always so unpleasant . . . and besides, we've wasted too much time already.

MRS. WATERS. One moment more, please.

[MRS. WATERS *walks off* L *and returns immediately, escorting* FITZPATRICK, *who looks weak and has his arm in a sling.*]

MRS. WATERS. My lord, Mr. Fitzpatrick! [*A sensation in the court.*]

HARRIET. My husband!

LADY BELLASTON. Shh! Make believe he isn't there and he may go away.

FITZPATRICK [*a broken man*]. Me gentle Harriet.

DOWLING. Then you are not dead?

FITZPATRICK. No.

DOWLING [*wisely*]. That's very important evidence.

FITZPATRICK. The doctor who attended me was young and inexperienced. When he told me I would die, I regretted me rash temper . . . and to what straits it had led this gentleman who was surely innocent of any evil . . . and I regretted me behavior to me wife to whom I have certainly acted the beast. I want to mend me ways if she will have me back.

HARRIET [*in tears*]. Fitzpatrick! [*Rushes to him.*]

FITZPATRICK. Harriet! [*They embrace.*]

DOWLING [*wiping away a tear*]. Touching. Case dismissed. Get them all out of here and let's get on with the next murderer!

ALLWORTHY. Wait! There is one thing more to be settled. You, Tom, are now my only heir.

TOM. You are too good to me.

ALLWORTHY. I always have been. But now you are my heir, I cannot think that Mr. Western will have any objections to a match between you and Miss Sophia.

WESTERN. Oh, I always loved the boy! To her, Tom, go to her! [TOM *crosses toward* SOPHIA, *who moves away from him to the other side of her father.*]

SOPHIA. I am in all things obedient, sir, but I do not wish to marry Mr. Jones.

WESTERN. That's a woman! When I forbid her it was nothing but sighing and whining and rebellion, and now I'm for it, she's against it.

TOM. I prithee, madam, forgive me and make me the happiest man alive.

SOPHIA. Sir, you have been inconstant and so frequently and in so short a time.

TOM. I had no hope ever again to be able to throw myself at your feet as I do now—[*Throws himself face down at her feet and talks into the floor, making his speech indistinguishable.*]—but I was desperate at the thought . . .

SOPHIA. I can't hear you.

TOM [*rising again*]. My proposal to Lady Bellaston sprang only from a desire to keep her friendship that I might again find you. The lady herself has absolutely no charm for me.

LADY BELLASTON. Outrageous! I will never do good works for the poor again!

TOM. As for the woman at Upton, she could have been my mother.

PARTRIDGE. 'Tis true, I always thought she was.

TOM. Tell me, tell me I may hope.

SOPHIA [*coyly*]. What would my father have me do?

WESTERN. Why, girl, give him your hand at once. We've missed a week's good hunting already.

SOPHIA. I am in all things obedient to your wishes, father . . . and . . . [*Taking it from her purse.*] . . . I just happen to have my veil with me.

TOM [*embracing her*]. Sophia!

ALLWORTHY [*crossing to* DOWLING]. And can you marry them?

DOWLING [*testily*]. Yes! Yes! If they make haste. I am hours behind in my calendar. [MISS WESTERN *helps* SOPHIA *adjust her veil. The lovers cross to the Judge's bench and as he begins to read the service in pantomime,* PARTRIDGE *walks down to the audience.*]

PARTRIDGE. And so you see it is a pleasant story which ends happily with the lovers united and points a moral . . . though I myself could not tell you what it is. But it was surely worth your attention for an evening and as Master Shakespeare said, "All's well that ends well," and I hope your honors will find your own lives and loves end as well as our play.

DOWLING. I now pronounce you man and wife. [TOM *and* SOPHIA *kiss.*]

PARTRIDGE. Sweet? Good night, my lords and ladies and all gentlefolk.

CURTAIN

NOTES ON COSTUMES

While this play takes place in 1750, if the costumes are too difficult or expensive for your production, the play can be performed in modern dress or rehearsal clothes with the insertion of the optional line in Partridge's first speech in Act One.

Gentlemen in this period customarily wore knee breeches, long stockings, waistcoats and coats. Shirts with cravats. Wigs would be appropriate on some of the characters but not necessary except in two instances. If there are no wigs on the ladies, however, try to avoid obviously modern hair styles. The servants wear simple hair styles, pulled back severely or hanging uncurled. The ladies have elaborately curled hair.

TOM: Act One: Knee breeches in some dark color, a white shirt. On his re-entrance after fight scene, he also wears a cravat and a waistcoat and coat matching his breeches. Act Two: The same. Act Three: The same. After the Lady Bellaston scene, change to light, colorful city clothes, much more elegant than his earlier costume. At this point he should add a white powdered wig and a sword.

SOPHIA: Act One: She wears a light, simple dress in a cheerful color. A fur muff. Act Two: A dark cape over her dress. Act Three: When she returns from the theatre a change to a more elaborate silk town dress would be effective but is not essential. In the last scene she puts on a simple wedding veil.

WESTERN: He wears a wool suit in some plain gray or brown color. He too can change to a town suit for Act Three but this is not essential. If available, he might wear a large, very curly, mangy wig.

MISS WESTERN: She is a Londoner and wears a more elaborate dress of richer material. For the road scene in Act Two, she adds a cape. A change of gown for Act Three and a curled wig would be effective but not necessary. She usually carries a fan.

ALLWORTHY: Act One: He wears a simple dark suit, and if a wig is used, a simple, unpowdered one. In his second appearance in Act One, he does not wear the wig and appears in a nightgown and cap. In his fourth appearance in Act One, when he has left his sick bed, a robe may be added over the nightgown. Act Three: The same or another simple, dark suit.

JENNY JONES (MRS. WATERS): Act One: As a serving girl, Jenny wears a dark dress or a long skirt and blouse. They are dirty and patched. Her face is dirty and her hair is matted and uncombed. Act Two: She wears a torn skirt and blouse, but her hair is now dressed and she is wearing makeup. She is dirtied from her struggle. An effort should be made to make her look as different from her Act One appearance as possible. On her third appearance in Act Two, she wears a dark simple dress such as Mrs. Whitefield would own; her face is clean and her hair combed. Act Three: She wears an elaborate town dress and hairdo or wig, high makeup including beauty spots.

PARTRIDGE: He wears a simple suit in a plain color and material.

BLIFIL: He wears a dark suit and sallow makeup throughout. If a wig is used, it should be a simple, dark one.

DOWLING: Acts One and Two: He wears a simple black suit. Act Three: He appears in an English judge's robe and wig.

HARRIET: She appears in a town dress and hairdo. In Act Two and the first scene of Act Three, she wears a cape over her dress.

FITZPATRICK: He wears one suit, either town or country, a sword, and a wig if desired.

LADY BELLASTON: The most fashionable lady, she should have the most elaborate town dress and powdered wig if possible. She wears a high makeup with beauty marks and jewels.

SQUARE, THWACKUM *and* DOCTOR: Simple dark suits are appropriate.

CAPTAIN BLIFIL: He wears a simple dark suit or Army uniform of the period if available.

CONSTABLE: He wears a simple dark suit or uniform of the period if available.

HIGHWAYMAN: He wears a suit entirely covered by a long, black cape. (If he is doubled, suit from other character can be used.) Mask, three-cornered hat, and pistol.

HONOUR: Act One: Plain gray dress, apron. Small fur muff for first scene. During Act Two, Scene One, she adds a cape. Act Three: She removes cape and apron.

BRIDGET: She wears a plain dark dress.

MRS. WHITEFIELD: She wears a plain dark dress, and an apron if desired.

DEBORAH, SUSAN *and* NANCY: The serving women wear plain simple dresses in dark color—black, brown, dark green or the like—or long dark skirts and simple blouses. Aprons if desired.

MALE SERVANTS (if used): Dark breeches and plain shirts.

PROPERTIES

GENERAL: Act One: Cutouts of two English manor houses, small stool. Wooden table, two chairs, bench, a few chairs or small sofa, table, small bed on wheels. Act Two: Three doors on wheels (see Production Notes), cutout tree and moon. Sophia's room: Small dressing table and chair, Sophia's muff, clothes tree with two women's capes; large scarf, jewels and clothing in drawer of table. Inn at Upton: Large table, stools, quill pen and paper on large table, small table and stool, small table and two chairs, two stools. Lady Bellaston's drawing room: Sofa or love seat, chair, small table, bell on table, writing table and chair, quill pen and paper on writing table. Courtroom: Judge's bench, chair.

PARTRIDGE: Knapsack, Sophia's muff (Act Two).

BRIDGET: Baby wrapped in blanket.

SQUIRE ALLWORTHY: Baby wrapped in blanket, piece of paper.

CAPTAIN BLIFIL: Ring.

BLIFIL: Book, handkerchief, black-bordered handkerchief.

TOM: Piece of wood, knife, sling for arm (Act One); knapsack, large wooden staff, Sophia's muff (Act Two); waistcoat, coat, wig, sword, note, note in pocket (Act Three).

WESTERN: Pistol (Act One); large old-fashioned key, pistol (Act Two).

SOPHIA: Muff, coins (Act Two); large purse containing wedding veil (Act Three).

MISS WESTERN: Folding fan.

HONOUR: Sophia's muff (Act One); tray with two plates and mug on it, small bag, luggage (Sophia's scarf-wrapped bundle, etc.), Sophia's muff (Act Two); note, another note (Act Three).

JUSTICE DOWLING: Gavel.

HIGHWAYMAN: Pistol, mask, purse.

HARRIET: Traveling bag, handkerchief.

FITZPATRICK: Coins, teacup.

SUSAN: Tray of food, dustcloth, towel; tray with two plates of rib roast (with bones), silverware, mugs, napkins.

NANCY: Mirror, note.